This is a mistake, Krystle thought, as her body heated and she gave in to desire for the man who held her in his arms. You know it is. Damn it, stop…

But she couldn't. It made no sense. It wasn't like her to let go like this, not with someone she hardly knew, and yet she couldn't stop herself, couldn't pull back.

Didn't *want* to.

She didn't understand what it was about Zack McIntyre that fired up her attraction.

All she knew was she needed this, *wanted* this. Needed to feel like a woman again. The hired killer who has been pursuing her for so long had robbed her of so much, including her feelings. She hadn't allowed herself to feel *anything,* all these long months. She desperately wanted something, at least one thing, back—if only for a few precious minutes.

She wanted to *feel* again.…

Dear Reader,

June brings you four high-octane reads from Silhouette Romantic Suspense, just in time for summer. Steaming up your sunglasses is Nina Bruhns's hot romance, *Killer Temptation* (#1516), which is the first of a thrilling new trilogy, SEDUCTION SUMMER. In this series, a serial killer is murdering amorous couples on the beach and no lover is safe. You won't want to miss this sexy roller coaster ride! Stay tuned in July and August for Sheri WhiteFeather's and Cindy Dees's heart-thumping contributions, *Killer Passion* and *Killer Affair*.

USA TODAY bestselling author Marie Ferrarella enthralls readers with *Protecting His Witness* (#1515), the latest in her family saga, CAVANAUGH JUSTICE. Here, an undercover cop crosses paths with a secretive beauty who winds up being a witness to a mob killing. And then, can a single mother escape her vengeful ex *and* fall in love with her protector? Find out in Linda Conrad's *Safe with a Stranger* (#1517), the first book in her miniseries, THE SAFEKEEPERS, which weaves family, witchcraft and danger into an exciting read. Finally, crank up your air-conditioning as brand-new author Jill Sorenson raises temperatures with *Dangerous to Touch* (#1518), featuring a psychic heroine and lawman, who work on a murder case and uncover a wild attraction.

This month is all about finding love against the odds and those adventures lurking around every corner. So as you lounge on the beach or in your favorite chair, lose yourself in one of these gems from Silhouette Romantic Suspense!

Sincerely,

Patience Smith
Senior Editor

MARIE FERRARELLA

Protecting His Witness

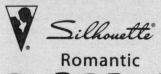

Romantic
SUSPENSE

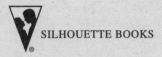

SILHOUETTE BOOKS

ISBN-13: 978-0-373-27585-4
ISBN-10:   0-373-27585-4

PROTECTING HIS WITNESS

Books by Marie Ferrarella

MARIE FERRARELLA

This *USA TODAY* bestselling and RITA® Award-winning author has written more one hundred and fifty books for Silhouette, some under the name Marie Nicole. Her romances are beloved by fans worldwide.

To
families everywhere,
and to my own small circle.
What would I ever do without
you?

Chapter 1

He could sense the blood leaving his body.

His hand turned sticky where he pressed it against his side and he began to feel dangerously light-headed.

With effort, Zack McIntyre forced himself to focus on his end goal: to get away and find help.

He cursed himself for letting this happen, but who would have expected to be jumped in the alley right behind an Internet café? Especially in an upscale neighborhood. When the man he'd been following had slipped out the back a minute before the owner closed down, Zack had been about a minute behind him.

Once outside, he was jumped. The confrontation—and ultimate end result—had been unavoidable.

The alleyway had been deserted. At eleven o'clock,

he had no doubts that most of the people who lived around here were already home, most likely in bed. He'd fled, bleeding, before anyone else showed up.

The shop was located at the tail end of a small strip mall nestled on the corner of a not-so-frequented thoroughfare. Facing the street, it was flanked on three sides by three separate housing developments. Zack had managed to escape into the smallest one, all while doing his best not to pass out. Whimsically named Stonehenge, the development was comprised of tiny, cookie-cutter white brick houses sealed two or three to a package, their backs all turned to a common alley.

It was through this alley that he found himself weaving.

Weaving badly.

Zack strained to hear the sound of approaching sirens. All he heard were crickets searching for love and companionship. That meant no one had found the body. Yet.

His side felt as if it was on fire.

Looking down, he was surprised there weren't any flames radiating between his fingers as he continued pressing against the wound. Blood kept seeping along his palm.

All attempts at calling this in had failed. There was a radio tower not too far off. That and the power lines crackling along the right-of-way in the damp night air played havoc with cell phone signals, imprisoning them within their phones.

Nothing was coming or going.

Just his luck.

Par for tonight. The car he was using had had two of its tires slashed. No getaway there.

Zack staggered and nearly fell, face forward. It was hard holding on to consciousness when his head was spinning so badly. It felt as if the edges were slipping through his fingers. Everything was exceedingly blurry and out of focus.

He needed help.

Arriving at one door, clutching his side with one hand, he pounded on a door with the other. When that yielded nothing, he tried another door. And another.

No one answered. No one stirred. Either he'd somehow managed to stumble into a ghost development, or people had finally learned not to open their doors after eleven at night.

Good for them, he thought. Bad for him.

"I should have arranged to get shot at noon," Zack muttered to himself. Everything in his head became progressively jumbled.

Damn it, somebody had to be home, someone had to answer their door. He just needed one person, just one. That and a first-aid kit.

Hell, he could do without the person as long as he had the kit. He wasn't Rambo, but he knew enough to be able to stitch up his own wound.

As long as he didn't lose any more blood.

Somehow, he made it to yet another back door. His fist outstretched to try to rouse whoever lived inside, Zack stumbled again, the toe of his boot hitting uneven gravel. This time, he pitched forward as the darkness around him descended, moving in closer until it merged with the growing darkness within.

And then there was nothing.

Kasey eased her small car around the corner, getting off the main drag and weaving in and out of the small, honeycomb-like streets that eventually fed into the area where she lived. As far as houses went, these left a lot to be desired. The small development was filled with either young couples just starting out, or older people who'd gleefully slipped out of the rat race and had only a few basic requirements in their lives: shelter and quiet.

But beggars and their kind couldn't be choosers.

Hers was the smallest model, with only one bedroom, one bath, a tiny living room and an even tinier kitchen. There was no sense pretending a family room or dining room existed. In a practical sense, this suited her purposes just fine. She could almost see everything in one long, sweeping glance as long as the bedroom door was open. No one could hide here. No one could surprise her.

Which was just the way she liked it.

In addition to the condo, she also had a tiny, one-car garage nestled in between two other, slightly bigger garages, each belonging to one of the houses on either side of hers. At a quick glance, it almost looked as if the other two garages were trying to squeeze hers out of existence.

A lot of that going around lately, she mused.

Kasey shook her head as she hit the automatic

garage-door opener. That was just her paranoia speaking up. Being tired did that to her. There was no reason to feel paranoid here. She was safe. At least as safe as she could be under the circumstances.

The second she didn't feel that way, she'd move. Again. And God knew, she didn't like the prospect of having to move yet one more time. She'd already moved three times since the incident.

Three times, to three different towns, desperately trying to feel safe again. This last time she'd finally come to the conclusion that there was no such thing as safe, not for her. At least, not completely. This was as good as it got.

She'd been here in Aurora for eight months. So far, so good.

Lining up her vehicle before the opened garage, she was about to pull in, but then something at the last moment stopped her. She didn't want the car inaccessible, even for a moment. What made tonight different from last night and the nights before, she didn't know. Maybe she was more tired tonight, but she'd learned to go with her instincts. It had saved her from a bullet last time.

So, rather than park her car inside the barren garage, she left the vehicle several feet away, sitting beside the curb that bordered the development. It wasn't that far from her back door—if she needed it in a hurry.

Still sitting inside the vehicle, she sighed. "You've got to stop this," she murmured under her breath. "It's been over eight months and no one's come after you."

The fact that no one had—to her knowledge—was a relief, but not enough to put her at ease. There were days that she sincerely doubted she would *ever* be at ease again, ever allow herself to reclaim the easygoing person she'd once been. Reclaim the life she'd once had. The life she'd worked so hard to achieve.

It could be worse, she thought ruefully, annoyed at the wave of self-pity that had claimed her. She could be dead.

Like Jim.

"No," she upbraided herself. "Not tonight."

She couldn't think about Jim tonight. Couldn't think about what happened that awful day her life changed forever. Tonight she just wanted to get out of her clothes and fall into bed. And with any luck, not dream about anything until it was time to get up again.

She wasn't feeling all that lucky.

The next moment, she had good reason not to. As she was about to head toward the back door that faced the alley, the chief feature that sold her on renting the tiny condo, Kasey caught her breath.

There was a form slumped across the single concrete step in front of her back door. She stood frozen, trying to make out the shape even as she tried to convince herself that it was just the moonlight playing tricks on her. That it wasn't what it looked like.

But it was.

It was a man.

Her first instinct was to run back to the car, get inside and lock all the doors. Had she not been who she was, from the shelter of her locked automobile she would have called the police and had them come out to deal with the man on her doorstep.

But she only took a few steps back and she didn't call the police. The police held more terror for her than the man who was slumped across the back entrance to her home.

Holding her breath, Kasey took a tentative step back. Then another. All the while her eyes never left the man on her doorstep. She watched for movement, for any sign of life.

The man didn't move a muscle.

Was he sleeping? Was this some poor, homeless creature who'd just given up the ghost, dying at her back door?

No, he was breathing, she could just barely see that. Staring at him, she noted the barest indication of his shoulders rising and falling.

He didn't look like a homeless man.

Even though the streetlamp lighting was far from the best, she could see that her uninvited guest was clean. Looking closer, she saw that his skin wasn't leathery. If he lived outdoors, it was a relatively new development.

"Hey, mister," she called out, doing her best not to allow her voice to tremble, "are you all right?"

There was no answer. As far as she could see, there wasn't even any indication that he had heard her. But she didn't relax.

He could be one of them. Could be playing "possum" just to get her to come in closer. If she knew what was good for her, she'd make a beeline for her car and head back to the bookstore that she'd just locked up.

Making up her mind, she was about to do exactly that when something on the ground caught her eye. There was a dark pool of liquid forming beside him. Beneath him. Kasey didn't have to guess what it was. She'd been part of this kind of scenario before.

Nerves came to attention as her heart leaped to her throat. Kasey scanned the area, trying to peer into the shadows. Was there someone else out there? Someone who had done this? Someone who was waiting for her?

But there appeared to be nothing to disturb the tranquility of the evening. Not even her neighbor's orange cat was out tonight. Ordinarily, Cymbeline was out, inspecting the area, looking for the occasional mouse that strayed from the right-of-way into the development.

It was almost too quiet.

Kasey wasn't sure if her training or just plain stupidity was to blame for her advancing several steps toward the man. She held her breath as she did so, as if that could somehow give her courage.

"Mister, you have to get up and go." When there was no response from the man, not even a change in his breathing, she tried again. This time, she spoke more authoritatively. And lied. "I've called the police. They'll be here any minute. So if you don't want to do your explaining to them, I suggest you stop playing around and get out of here."

Still nothing.

He was really unconscious. And bleeding.

So now what? she wondered, nervously chewing on her lower lip. She couldn't just circle around to the front entrance and forget about him. Pretend he wasn't there. No matter how much she felt she'd lost of herself these last two years, that compassionate part was still there. She wasn't cold-blooded.

She sighed. No, that wasn't what she was like, even though there were times that she felt that everything she'd ever been had died that day with Jim. Gunned down just like him.

Hesitantly, she stretched out her fingers and felt for a pulse at the man's throat. The moment she touched him, his eyes opened and he grabbed her wrist.

Kasey swallowed a scream as she jerked her hand out of his grasp. The fact that she could do so easily told her that the man was definitely weak. Someone that big, that strong-looking would have easily held on to her if he wanted to no matter how hard she pulled—if he wasn't being impeded by a debilitating wound.

"Help me."

The entreaty, hardly above a whisper, slipped from his lips and seemed to fade almost immediately into the dark night. But she'd definitely heard it. Heard, too, the desperate note behind the words.

His eyes had closed again.

Kasey blew out a breath, torn. Again she thought about calling the police. But what if he was running from the police? If she got them to come here, she definitely wouldn't be doing this man any favors.

So now you're helping out felons?

The question ricocheted in her head, taunting her. But what if he wasn't a felon? And what if circumstances were such that he didn't want the police? After all, wasn't she in essence running from the police—from certain members of the police force? And she certainly wasn't a felon. If anything, she was a victim. Just someone who wanted to live to see another Christmas.

C'mon, make up your mind. Do something. Doing nothing was not an option. If she just turned her back and left him here, this man could very well bleed to death and she would be as guilty of his murder as if she'd pulled a trigger.

There were only two options. She either called the police, or did something for the stranger herself.

Kasey ventured a glance at the stranger's face. He didn't look like a bad guy, she thought. And if he did turn out to be one, well, it wasn't as if she was completely defenseless. There was a gun inside the largest canister on her kitchen counter, right beside the ones containing flour, sugar and tea.

She'd actually practiced getting the weapon out under adverse conditions—just in case. Jim would have laughed at her if he could have seen her.

But then, she thought ruefully, as sadness strummed through her again, if he could have seen her, there would have been no reason to have a loaded gun hidden in the largest canister on her counter.

The stranger's eyes were still closed.

And he was still bleeding.

Kasey made up her mind. She had the training and she could help him, the way she couldn't help Jim.

Unlocking her door, she gingerly stepped over him to enter her house. Once inside, she turned around. She was going to bring him in.

"Okay, mister, this is your lucky night. But I promise you, if you try anything—anything at all—it'll also be your last night."

The stranger opened his eyes again and looked at her. She couldn't begin to fathom what he was thinking. The next moment, he tried to struggle to his feet. Kasey had the feeling that if she blew on him, he'd fall backward like a stack of cards.

"Hold it," she cautioned before he could do any damage to himself. "This is going to be a team effort." Tossing aside her purse, Kasey squatted down beside him. "Give me your arm."

Not waiting for him to comply, she draped his arm around the back of her neck herself. Holding tightly on to it, she placed her other arm around his waist as best she could. To gain a better grasp, she slid her fingers through the belt loop of his jeans. She hoped the loop would hold when she needed it.

Kasey took another deep breath, bracing herself. "Okay, on the count of three, I want you to try to get up, understand?"

He made some kind of noise in response. "I'll take that as a yes." Ready to push off, she counted, "One, two, *three.*"

She only managed to get a couple of inches off the ground before the stranger threw her off balance. Caught off guard, she fell over on him.

Instantly, Kasey drew back. Had he done that on purpose? She tried to give him the benefit of the doubt, but trusting no longer came easily to her.

"You're going to have to do better than that," she told him.

There was no answer. She realized that the stranger was unconscious again and deadweight. She sighed. "Not going to make this easy for either of us, are you?"

She needed another approach. Rising to her feet, she got behind him and put her arms around his chest. She laced her hands together and pulled him across the threshold and along the floor.

Progress was made by inches but she had always prided herself on her strength and even in these dire times—or maybe because of them—she worked out religiously, concentrating on weight training and building up her upper body strength.

Finally getting all of him inside her small house, Kasey felt like collapsing. Not only was the man deadweight, he was rock solid. But rather than take a breather, she straightened up and turned on the closest light. No way would she voluntarily stay in the dark with this man. Closing the door, she turned around to face her uninvited guest. There was a very disconcerting trail of blood leading from the threshold to the living room.

She was going to have to clean that up before the bloodstains set in permanently. But first, she had to stop the blood at its source.

Kasey glanced over her shoulder. Her sofa was only a few feet away from the back door, but it might as well have been in the next county. Even if she managed to pull him the distance, she wouldn't be able to get him onto the sofa. At least, not without going through extraordinary contortions and she was much too tired for that.

Which meant she had to treat him on the floor. Everything in her training balked at that, but you couldn't always pick your settings.

"Not exactly the ideal conditions," she murmured to herself. She laid him flat on his back. "Who are you and why are you here?" she couldn't help wondering aloud.

Well, there was time enough to learn that later, once she stopped the bleeding and sewed up his wound. Despite the situation, a small thrill raced through her. It had been much too long since she'd done anything close to her profession—and she missed it. Missed her life. Missed a lot of things.

She hurried off to the bathroom to wash her hands and to get what she needed in order to take care of this man that fate, with its sardonic sense of humor, had deposited on her doorstep.

She couldn't help the dry laugh that rose to her lips. The way her luck had been going this last year and a half, the man on her floor would probably turn out to be a serial killer. Wouldn't take much for her to be his next victim.

Drying her hands, she started throwing things she was going to need into the small, pink rubber basin she kept under the sink: alcohol, swabs, a scalpel and sutures she kept in a small blue container on the top shelf of her medicine cabinet.

Being his next victim might not be so bad, she mused. It might even be a blessing in disguise. She was weary of hiding, weary of looking over her shoulder so often. Maybe, if he repaid her act of kindness by killing her, at least this awful game of hide-and-seek would be over and she'd finally know some peace. Know what it was like not to have her heart leap up, hammering wildly with anxiety every time the door to the bookstore opened, or she looked up to see someone looking her way. She was tired of all the paranoia. If she couldn't have her life back, she didn't want any life at all.

You're just tired and not making any sense, she chided herself ruefully.

If she meant any of that, she wouldn't be double-locking her door, or taking all those precautions every day. Maybe this life she led wasn't so great, but it certainly did beat the alternative. At bottom, she wanted to live. And live long enough to get the person who had killed Jim and tried to kill her.

After checking to make sure she had everything she needed, for now she focused on her patient. Kasey didn't have to look in the mirror to know that, as uneasy as she was, she was still smiling.

The smile faded the moment she stepped out into the living room again.

There was no one lying on the floor by the back entrance.

Chapter 2

For one frantic moment, Kasey thought the stranger had either left, or, worse, lay in wait for her somewhere in the house.

But then she saw him. It took a second for her heart to stop pounding as she realized that the stranger had just moved. He was still on the floor, but now closer to the kitchen. She guessed that he must have come to, tried to get up and collapsed when he found that the effort was too much for him.

But why the kitchen? Why hadn't he tried to go out the door?

"You were probably disoriented," she said under her breath as she crossed to him. She knelt down, setting the basin with its supplies next to her. "I can certainly relate to that."

Every day, when she first woke up, she had to take stock of where she was and who she was. There were times when it all felt so jumbled up in her brain, she wanted to give up running, give up hiding and just return to her old life.

Which, she guessed, she'd probably be allowed to live for a total of ten minutes before word got around that she was back and among the living. And someone decided to do something about the latter.

Was that who this man was on her floor? Someone running from something?

Or was this an elaborate plan to flush her out, she wondered, her fingertips growing icy. Someone sent to get her, once and for all. She knew there was always a chance of that, but getting shot just to lull her into a false sense of security seemed like quite a stretch.

When you hear hoofbeats, think horses, not zebras. It was one of the mantras she'd been taught in medical school and it applied not just to the field, but to life. The unconscious man in her living room was probably a horse, not a zebra. Some poor victim, not a hit man.

And if he was to continue being a horse, she had to help him live. And pretty damn quick.

She raised his blood-soaked shirt away from his body. It was a bullet wound all right. Right there just under his arm. She'd seen worse, but there was no such thing as a good bullet wound. Slipping on a pair of plastic gloves she'd picked up at the local drugstore, she took a sterile swab, soaked it in peroxide and proceeded to clean the wound.

With each stroke, Kasey raised her eyes and watched the unconscious stranger's face with apprehension. But there was no reaction, no indication that he was only pretending to be unconscious. No involuntary wincing. He was out cold.

"Lucky for both of us," she murmured. "I'm probably a little rusty at this."

The wound cleaned, she reached for the scalpel she'd scrubbed less than five minutes ago.

Poising the blade over the bullet's point of entry, she told him, "This is going to be the hard part." Still nothing.

Which was good. But she still wished she had something to knock the man out in case he woke up and began to struggle. But things like that, other than 101 proof whiskey, couldn't be purchased in the local pharmacy. Besides, she honestly never thought she'd need something in the way of an anesthetic ever again. She'd left that life behind, not willingly, but of necessity. It all boiled down to the same thing. She wasn't a practicing doctor anymore.

Very carefully, she began to probe the wound. Glancing up at the stranger's face, she saw him tense even though he was in another realm where hard-core pain didn't exist. Her patient continued sleeping. Satisfied that, at least for the time being, he was unaware of what was happening, she probed deeper. Just where had this bullet gone?

After a couple more minutes, she was finally rewarded with the feel of metal against metal.

Gotcha.

Holding her breath, she secured the bullet and gingerly retracted the instrument until she could pull it free of the flesh around it.

Like a fisherman who had managed to finally pull a marlin out of the water, she held up the tiny bit of mangled metal, examining it against the overhead light. She shook her head.

"Not much to look at, is it?" she marveled. Small but deadly was an apt description. She wondered if the man on the floor knew how close he came to never seeing another sunrise. "Bet that could have ended your life with no effort at all if it'd hit just a little bit higher and to the left. Talk about lucky…"

Again she shook her head, awed how some people died after tripping on the sidewalk and hitting their head, while others walked away from what appeared to be certain death after taking a fall from a second-story window. Or catching a bullet just beneath their rib cage, she thought, amazed.

Cleaning the wound a second time, Kasey then picked up the sutures and very carefully sewed up the small hole. She wished she had access to some antibiotics to insure against infections, but he would have to take care of that for himself. Once he was awake.

It didn't take long to finish stitching him up, even though she took her time, studying his face after every stitch was taken.

"You really are dead to the world, aren't you?" she

marveled. Finished, she put what was left of the sutures into a small white envelope and sealed it again.

There wasn't much.

"Now what?" she asked herself out loud, looking down at her patient.

He was still unconscious, still in her house. What did she do with him? She had no one to turn to, no one to go to for help. And that was strictly her own doing. Edwin Owens, the owner of the used bookstore Rare Treasures, had indicated that he was very willing to be her friend. Very willing to be more than that if she wanted him to be. But while he seemed like a nice man, she knew better than to make friends or form attachments. Friends asked questions, they noticed things about you. Things they could repeat, however innocently, to people who might come looking for you.

So this was better, remaining an isolated mystery. It was also far less complicated. Now that she thought about it, this path she'd been forced to choose was also a great deal more lonely. Until right this minute, loneliness had not been a real problem for her. God knew she had more than enough on her mind to keep her occupied and busy. Too busy to feel lonely.

But right now, if not an actual shoulder to lean on, she could have really used an extra pair of hands to help her with this man.

Blowing out a long breath, Kasey shrugged as she put everything back into the basin and went back to the bathroom with it. There was no point in dwelling on what she didn't have. She would have to make the best of it.

The way she had these last endless months.

Switching off the bathroom light, she went to the minuscule linen closet next. It was hardly big enough to hold a handful of towels and the extra bedding she kept there for cold winter nights. Grabbing the pink flannel blanket and the lone pillow from the top shelf, she returned to her patient.

On her knees, Kasey gently raised his head and slipped the pillow under it, then threw the flannel blanket over him. She spread it out, making sure all of him was covered.

"Who are you?" she asked softly as she rose again to her feet.

He'd had no wallet on him, no ID. She'd already checked his pockets. Had he been mugged? Or was there some other reason he didn't have any identification with him?

Too many questions, no answers, she thought.

Looking down at herself, Kasey realized that she'd gotten the stranger's blood on her when she'd dragged him in as well as on the floor and her rug. It wasn't going to scrub itself out. So, for the next forty-five minutes, she did what she could to wash the telltale streaks of blood from her house and herself.

When she was finally finished with that, she paused to check the lock on the bathroom door. Satisfied that it would hold, she still brought in a chair. Closing the door, she wedged the chair underneath the doorknob—just in case. She'd learned the hard way that trusting made you exceptionally vulnerable.

Kasey took the world's fastest shower.

Coming out of the bathroom, dressed in a pair of jeans and a fresh shirt, still relatively damp from the shower, she checked on the stranger one more time. This time, he was exactly where she'd left him and he was still unconscious. The body was doing its part to help him heal.

As for her, she knew that her body was far too keyed up now to sleep. Resigned to yet another restless night, not unlike so many other nights, Kasey staked out a place for herself on the sofa, turned the TV on to one of the classic cable channels and turned the sound down to a whisper. She didn't really need to hear what was being said. She knew the dialogue to this particular movie by heart. Even so, there was a certain amount of comfort in hearing the familiar repeated.

She smiled as Cary Grant, resplendent in a tuxedo and radiating charm, came on the scene. Some things you could always count on. It made her feel a tad better.

He felt as if his body had been disassembled and then put back together incorrectly, with some of the parts missing. Every single bone and muscle in his body made its presence known with one hell of an ache.

But pain was a good thing, right? Pain meant he was alive.

Either that or in hell.

With effort, Zack pried open his eyes. The first thing that came into focus was the flannel blanket.

He was no expert, but he was fairly certain that there

were no pink blankets in hell. Which meant that his first impression was right. He was alive.

It was a good starting point.

He played dead for a moment, lowering his eyelids until all that remained opened were two tiny slits. Zack scanned the immediate area in front of him. He was lying on the floor of someone's house.

Whose?

And for that matter, what was he doing on the floor, covered with a blanket? It wasn't pulled over his head, so they—whoever "they" were—obviously didn't think that he was dead. But why had they brought him here?

And, while he was at it, just where was *here?*

And what the hell was that searing pain all about? It threatened to take off the top of his head. The only way he could have felt worse was if he'd fallen headfirst into a wood chipper.

Zack struggled to extract his brain from the center of its cotton-batting prison. He needed to think clearly in order to piece things together.

He thought back. The last thing he remembered was going out into the alley behind the Internet café.

No, wait, the *last* thing he remembered was being shot and struggling with the man he'd been tailing. He'd tried to get possession of the man's weapon before he could get off another shot. But it did go off again. And this time, the bullet had gone into the other man's body.

Had it killed him?

Zack didn't know. He always hit what he aimed for

but this time, he wasn't aiming. The discharge had been by accident, forced by the other man's hand.

No, wait, that *wasn't* the last thing he remembered, he amended again, desperately trying to hang on to loose, stray thoughts. He remembered trying to get away. He *did* get away. He'd managed to leave the strip mall and find his way into a development of white brick houses. A whole village of them. It was like something out of that silly fairy tale about the three little pigs. Except that he wasn't the big bad wolf.

Even so, when he'd knocked on one door after another, nobody would let him in. No one would help him. And then, too weak to go on, he'd fallen to his knees before the last house.

After that, there was nothing. Had he passed out?

There was a woman on the sofa, dozing from the looks of it. Did he know her? He didn't think so. He would have remembered a woman who looked like this one did, he thought. Even from this distance, with his eyes all but shut, he could see the woman with the curly brown hair had class. And looks.

Too bad he wasn't going to meet her, but he really had to get out of here. There was someplace he had to be by noon. Dawn was breaking, so he judged that he still had some time left. But he had a feeling he wasn't exactly himself today and that getting to where he had to be would require a lot of energy. If he didn't make it in time, all hell could break loose. He knew that without being told. This was a delicate operation that required precise timing.

Removing the blanket from his body with a hand that felt incredibly stiff, Zack started to sit up.

The flash of sharp, excruciating pain was completely unexpected. So was the moan that involuntarily escaped his lips.

The woman on the sofa was awake and on her feet before he realized that the sound had come from him.

She had long, curly light brown hair and blue eyes that flashed as she came closer.

"What are you doing?" she demanded sharply, crossing to him.

He would have thought that would have been obvious. "Trying to get up."

"Wait," she cautioned, putting a hand on his shoulder to stop him. She squatted down beside him. "Put your arm around my shoulders."

Why did that sentence sound so familiar to him? As if he'd just heard it moments ago. But that was impossible. He had a feeling he'd been out at least several hours.

Shaking off any extraneous thoughts, he tried to do the same with the woman. "I can get up by myself," he told her.

"No, you can't." She said it with such authority, he almost believed her. "If you strain yourself, you'll wind up breaking open your stitches." Her tone left no room for argument. "Now, lean on me and let me help."

No matter what she sounded like, the woman looked like a delicate little thing. Just proved that looks could be deceiving. The strength he felt in her hands as she wrapped one around his waist surprised him.

Though he hated to admit it, even to himself, getting up was a lot easier with her help.

She got him up and onto the sofa. But he didn't want to sit, he wanted to leave. Had to leave. Still, he was grateful for the momentary respite. Just getting to his feet had taken a lot out of him. He wasn't used to playing the invalid.

Breathing hard, he mumbled, "Thanks." After a beat, his breathing more regulated, he asked her, "How did I get here?"

She watched his face as she answered, looking for some telltale sign that this was a ruse. So far, he seemed genuinely confused. "I found you on my doorstep and dragged you inside."

Zack frowned. "Why didn't you call the police?" That would have been what most people would have done—if they would have done anything at all. If this had happened in one of the more metropolitan areas, the good citizens of that city would have probably walked right by him, pretending not to notice that he needed help.

She saw no reason to embellish on the truth. "You were bleeding and had a bullet wound. I didn't know if calling the police would have gotten you into more trouble."

"More?" he echoed.

"You were wounded," she pointed out. "That seemed like enough trouble for one person for the time being." She saw him glancing down at his side. Raising his bloodstained shirt, he exposed the large gauze bandage that wrapped around his rib cage. "I took the bullet out," she explained matter-of-factly, second-guessing his next question.

He let the shirt drop back into place. "You a doctor?"

Kasey congratulated herself on not batting an eyelash. Instead, she nonchalantly shook her head. "No. I work in a secondhand bookstore."

He raised a perplexed eyebrow at her answer. "I don't follow."

"I do a lot of reading in my spare time," she elaborated, adding, "I particularly like reading medical books."

He supposed that made sense, in an odd sort of way. He couldn't argue with the fact that she'd taken out the bullet. He spotted it in the center of a coaster on the coffee table.

"Lucky for me you retained what you read," he commented, amused.

She merely nodded. Getting up off the sofa, Kasey glanced toward the window. The sun was up. Time for her to get ready for work even though she'd had approximately an hour's worth of sleep. The television set was still on, softly droning in the background. Someone was extolling the virtues of a newly developed body cream that did everything up to and including finding Prince Charming.

Turning off the set with her remote control, Kasey turned toward the man she'd helped.

Logically, she should be ushering him on his way. She'd taken out his bullet, sewed him up and let him sleep on her floor. It was time for him to go.

And yet, caring for him had awakened the person she'd once been. The person she liked. It prompted her to take another step into the world of kindness. A few more minutes wouldn't hurt, she silently argued. "Would you like something to eat?"

The moment she asked, Zack became aware of the gnawing pain in his belly. It wasn't giving him discomfort because he'd been shot. He was hungry. He tried to remember the last time he'd eaten. Was it yesterday morning? The night before that? Zack couldn't recall. His line of work didn't encourage sticking to any sort of a reliable schedule.

He nodded in response to her question. "Yeah. If you don't mind."

She moved toward the kitchen. "If I'd minded," she informed him, "then I wouldn't have offered."

The lady sounded tough as nails—or was that only the impression she wanted to give? His job had taught him to look beneath the surface and read between the lines. Something had struck him as off right from the moment he opened his eyes.

"Aren't you going to ask me any questions?" he asked, rising to his feet. He was less steady than he would have liked and it hurt like hell to walk, but he figured each step would get easier.

Kasey stood before the pantry. "Do you want eggs or cereal?"

"Eggs." That wasn't the question he had in mind. "No, I mean about why I got shot."

She spared him a quick glance just before she opened

the refrigerator. She might have questions, but she
wasn't about to ask them.

"No," she told him, taking out the egg carton. "The
less I know, the less anyone else can ask me."

Chapter 3

Gingerly, bracing his hands on the small kitchen table, Zack lowered himself into the chair closest to him.

Maybe it was his police background, but he sensed she'd had experience with interrogation. She certainly piqued his curiosity, even if he did feel as if he'd been run over several times by a semi. Who was she? And was it chance, or fate, that had brought him literally to her doorstep?

"A woman with no curiosity," he marveled in awe. "I didn't think such a thing existed."

She set the carton of eggs on the counter. "I'm glad I could contribute to furthering your education."

No curiosity and a flippant response. An interesting combination. So was her long, curly light hair and her golden complexion. He watched the woman move gracefully around the small kitchen. No unnecessary movements. Everything seemed within reach. In moments, she had everything out and ready to prepare the breakfast she'd mentioned.

As he drew in the welcoming scent of coffee, she turned suddenly toward him. "How do you like your eggs?"

"Cooked."

His mouth quirked in a quick grin. It transformed a scruffy-looking possible criminal into an adolescent boy who knew his way around charming the opposite sex.

Wasted on me, hotshot, she thought. *I don't charm anymore.* But if she did, she added silently, that grin would have been an excellent start.

She waited for him to be more specific about his choice. When he wasn't, she pressed, "Any other requirements?"

Zack shook his head. "Nope, I'm easy. I'll have them whatever way you're having them. Fried, poached, scrambled…" His voice trailed off, leaving the rest up to her to fill in.

"Scrambled it is," she answered, turning back toward the counter and stove. Breaking four eggs, she dropped them directly into the frying pan rather than into a bowl. To her, it was just an unnecessary step, generating more dishes to wash. She took the spatula and broke apart the pattern the eggs began to form. The yolks and whites flowed into each other until they began to solidify in fluffy tufts. "Toast?"

Something he quite possibly would have been had she not been his Good Samaritan, Zack thought. He started to nod in response to her question, then realized that she wasn't looking at him. "If you don't mind."

This time she did spare him a glance over her shoulder. Her expression seemed to repeat her previous statement that if she'd minded, she wouldn't have asked him.

As she dropped two slices into the toaster, the silver appliance only held two slices. She was single, he decided. And had taken quite a chance with him.

"What's your name?" he asked suddenly.

Instead of answering, she looked over her shoulder at him again and asked, "Why?"

She might be short on curiosity, but she was long on suspicion, he thought. Was that inherent or something she'd learned? And if it was the latter, what had made her this way?

None of his thoughts were evident in his voice or on his face as he said glibly, "So that when I tell people the story of how an angel came to my rescue, I'll be able to refer to you by name."

Uh-huh, she thought. *Right.* She turned back to her cooking. "Rumplestiltskin."

Zack laughed. "Not hardly. You don't look like any ugly little fairy-tale creature that I ever saw in my sisters' storybooks."

So, he had sisters. Or was that just what he wanted her to think? God, but she missed the days when a duck was just a duck and not a camouflaged cheetah.

"That's just to give you a false sense of security," she told him.

Done, Kasey divided the eggs that were in the pan

between two plates. Just as she finished, the toast popped. After setting the frying pan down on a dormant burner, she took the toast and applied a light layer of margarine to both slices. She cut them in half at an angle and placed both onto the stranger's plate, framing the eggs. If she'd had bacon, she could have made a smiley face, like her mother used to a million years ago when both she and the world were innocent.

Kasey slid the plate in front of the dark-haired stranger. "There." She placed her own plate opposite his on the kitchen table. But instead of sitting down, she asked, "Coffee?"

He thought she'd never offer. His eyes darted toward the coffeemaker. "Just bring the pot."

She went to the cupboard and took out one cup, one mug. It was all she had. "Oh, you're one of those."

Watching her stretch to reach the top shelf made him momentarily forget about all the little devils beating on his body with pointy silver hammers. She had one hell of a graceful body, he couldn't help thinking.

"Those?" he queried when she turned around again.

Taking a little for herself—she only liked a small taste to get her going—she poured the rest into the large mug she ordinarily used when she sipped soup. "People who claim they can't wake up until they've had their morning coffee."

There were days when he felt as if he ran on coffee. "Guilty as charged."

Leaving her cup on the counter, she brought his mug over to him. "Milk, sugar?"

Zack shook his head, taking the mug from her and holding it with both hands, like someone receiving long-awaited sustenance.

"Only gets in the way," he told her. Zack took a deep drink and she could have sworn he sighed with contentment. Glancing up at her again, he said, "Good coffee."

"Grew the beans myself," she deadpanned, taking her seat. She saw his eyebrows knit themselves together in a bemused line. "The coffee comes from a can," she told him, erasing any misconceptions.

Obviously the man thought she had no sense of humor. Ordinarily, he would have been right. She had no idea what had possessed her to make the quip. Things like humor and kidding around had long since ceased being part of her daily life. She couldn't even begin to remember the last time she'd laughed. Running left no time for laughter, left nothing to even smile about.

With coffee in his veins and his belly, he felt almost human again. And ready to pick up where he'd left off. Trying to find out who she was. "You're really not going to tell me your name?"

She didn't look up from her plate. "Kasey," she answered. "Kasey Madigan."

"Well, Kasey, Kasey Madigan, it's an honor and a privilege to make your acquaintance." He put out his hand as if to shake hers.

Kasey kept her hand where it was. She nodded at his plate. "Just finish your breakfast. I have to leave soon and I can't have you here when I'm gone."

He could see her point. Nodding, Zack applied his fork to the fare before him.

He ate like a man who had only faint memories of his last meal. Quick and with gusto. Was he homeless? she wondered, going back to her initial impression of him. He was scruffy, but not that scruffy. The stubble on his face couldn't have been more than a couple of days old. If he was homeless, it couldn't have been for that long. But then, she supposed that even homeless people had a first week of homelessness in their past.

"Where do you work?"

He asked pleasantly enough, but she didn't like dealing with questions. *Any* kind of questions. "In a bookstore." She'd already told him that.

Zack nodded. "I know, but where is the bookstore located?"

"Why, are you looking to expand your library?" she asked.

She was reluctant to give out any information, he thought. And yet, she'd taken him in and seen to his wound, something a lot of other people wouldn't have done. Especially if they lived alone.

The woman seemed like a walking contradiction.

"You never know," he answered, going with her last comment. "I like reading."

She merely nodded, as if she expected everyone to feel that way about books. Zack let the topic drop. He noticed her plate was empty. The next second, she was getting up, taking it to the sink. He quickly polished off the last of his eggs and toast. He could have eaten more.

"This was good," he told her.

"It was simple," she replied, ignoring the compliment he had given her.

Leaning his palms against the table top, Zack slowly pushed himself up to his feet. Damn, he still felt wobbly. He had no patience with infirmity when he was the one who was infirm. This was going to be a problem, he thought.

Approaching her, he asked suddenly, "Do you have a car?"

She turned around from the sink and looked at him for a second, trying to read his expression before she answered. Did he want to take her car? If so, he was in no shape to drive.

"Yes." She let the single word hang in the air for a minute before asking, "Why?"

He didn't like asking for favors, especially from people he didn't know, but he needed to get back and Aurora's public transportation left a great deal to be desired.

"Look, you've already gone more than out of your way for me—"

She saw no reason to dispute that. "Yes."

He couldn't tell if she was agreeing with him, or tossing out the word just to make him get to the point faster. "I need a ride," he told her bluntly. "Someone slashed the tires on my car."

She wondered if it was actually his car, or if he'd stolen it. "Before or after they shot you?"

"Probably before." He stopped himself, his words replaying themselves in his head. "This sounds like some kind of melodrama, doesn't it?"

Her mouth curved slightly. "One that went straight to video," she agreed.

For a moment, Zack wrestled with his thoughts. He'd been undercover for several months now and things were obviously coming to a head. But his gut told him that this woman had no connections to the identity-theft ring he and his team were trying to break up. Wounded, bleeding and disoriented, he had come to her, she hadn't sought him out. That made her an outsider.

He didn't want to repay her act of kindness by telling her a lie. He really didn't have to tell her very much at all beyond a few nebulous pieces of information. At the very least, she deserved to know who she'd gone out of her way for.

"My name's Zack McIntyre."

"Okay," she said gamely. "Is that supposed to mean something to me?"

She really didn't want to know anything, did she? That either made her incredibly unique, or afraid of something. "No, but you didn't ask me what my name was after you told me yours."

Slender shoulders rose and fell in a careless shrug. "I figured if you wanted me to know, you'd tell me." She looked at him as if her point was made. "And you did."

Zack shook his head. His sisters could certainly take a few pointers from her. They acted as if they had the right to know every single detail of his life.

"You don't have any curiosity, do you?" he marveled.

"I know all I need to know to get me through the day," she replied complacently.

He didn't have to be a mind reader to know that as far as she was concerned, that was enough.

Zack watched her as she got ready to leave. "I'd be careful if I were you," he told her.

He was kidding, she told herself. But she still couldn't bank down the fear that suddenly spiked through her. Was he giving her a veiled warning? She succeeded in keeping her voice cool as she asked him, "And why's that?"

He watched as she slipped on her high heels. They gave her an extra four inches. "Well, a woman with no curiosity is a rare creature. Someone might be tempted to kidnap you and put you in a museum dedicated to rare and mythical creatures—like the unicorn."

Kasey slipped her purse straps onto her shoulder. "There are no such things as unicorns."

He winked at her as she crossed to the door. "Or so they'd like us to think."

It was just a simple little movement, a flutter of an eyelid. Why did that feel so unsettling? She hadn't even looked at another man since Jim had died. Hadn't even thought about anyone else. Where was this coming from?

It didn't matter where it was coming from, she upbraided herself sternly. What mattered was sending this man on his way, out of her life.

"Where do you want me to drop you off?" she asked as she opened the front door.

Home, Zack thought. Either the bachelor digs where he kept most of his clothes, or better yet, his mother's house where he and his brother and sisters had grown up. Just the sight of his mother would make him feel that God was in His heaven and all was right with the world. Especially now that Lila McIntyre was finally going to be marrying the man she should have been married to all along, her former partner and the current chief of detectives, Brian Cavanaugh. She would have had a much more peaceful life had she been Brian's wife and not his father's. They would *all* have had more peaceful lives if she'd married Brian instead.

Zack locked away the thought. No point in going there. And physically, he couldn't go to his mother's house anyway, not right now. Until he was told otherwise, until his captain pulled him off the case, he was still Danny Masters, a hacking genius with a talent for resurrecting information on so-called reformatted hard drives and with an unending need for other people's money.

So for now, he would return to the run-down motel room where he'd been staying for the duration of this charade. Because Danny Masters couldn't afford any better digs. Master computer wizard though he was and blessed with a silver tongue, he had one very bad fatal flaw. He gambled. On anything and anyone. Which made him the ideal employee for an unscrupulous employer. His addiction made him easier to control, easier to have power over. In essence, "Danny Masters" owed his soul to the company store.

He leaned against the whitewashed brick as he

waited for her to lock the front door. "I'll give you the address," he promised, "once we get into your car."

The look in her eyes was wary, as if she was debating whether or not to believe him. And then she seemed to make up her mind and nodded, tucking her purse under her arm.

"All right," she announced briskly, turning away from the house, "let's go."

Zack caught his lower lip between his teeth to suppress any sound of discomfort that might escape. His side really hurt. He fell into place beside his solemn angel of mercy, moving not nearly as quickly as he would have liked to.

But he was making progress, which was all that counted to him. His life and his job had taught him how to be a patient man.

Andrew Cavanaugh threw open the front door before his younger brother even took his finger off the doorbell. Brian had the keys to his house, as he had to Brian's, but an inherent respect for each other's privacy kept those keys in his pocket.

"We need to talk," Andrew declared, doing his best to harness the emotions that had prompted him to call and ask Brian to come over as quickly as possible.

"As I recall, you do that far better than me, big brother." Chief of Detectives Brian Cavanaugh braced himself as walked into his older brother's house.

The former chief of police had summoned him via a voice message that he'd left on his answering machine. Andrew's message, unlike his normal, friendly fare, was very somber. He hadn't a clue as to why.

Considering the fact that he and Lila McIntyre had given Andrew carte blanche to do whatever he wanted for their wedding reception, he would have expected his brother to be in fantastic spirits. Since leaving the force to care for his then-motherless brood of five, Andrew had turned his attention toward his second passion: cooking. Cooking was his way of keeping not just his immediate family but his *entire* family together. With one hand tied behind his back, the man could create huge, sumptuous meals for an amazing amount of people. No one who ever went to Andrew's house remained hungry once they crossed his threshold.

But one look at Andrew's face told Brian that this wasn't about food. Still, trying to keep the mood light and far too happy to allow himself to be brought down, Brian cracked, "What's the matter, the man doing the ice sculpture decide to back out?"

Andrew didn't even attempt to smile. Instead, he led the way to the kitchen and nodded toward a chair. "Sit down, Brian."

Something in Andrew's tone undercut any further attempt at humor. Andrew sounded just the way he had when he'd broken the news to him that their middle brother, Mike, had been killed in the line of duty.

They'd all followed in their father's footsteps and joined the force in their early twenties. Of the three of them, Mike had been the black sheep, the one who grew more and more resentful of the rut he found himself in. Andrew had done his best to keep Mike in line, to make him see and appreciate just how rich his life actually was. But Mike would have none of it, becoming envious as both his brothers received accolades and promotions while he remained a beat cop. Toward the end, there'd been hatred in Mike's eyes when he looked at them. Hatred because he felt he could never "measure up." Hatred mingled with self-loathing he'd tried to anesthetize with progressively more alcohol. All that did was generate even more problems.

Brian looked at his brother, trying to fathom whatever was coming. "I'll take whatever you have to say standing, Andrew."

This wasn't easy for him. Andrew had been the patriarch ever since a heart attack had claimed their father all those years ago. The patriarch and the voice of reason. After everything he'd been through in his life, he'd earned the right to expect tranquility, not turmoil, to fill the end of his days. But even beyond the grave, Mike managed to toss a little chaos their way.

"I had a visitor the other day," he began, searching for the right words. This was going to be a shock. Not just to Brian, but to Patrick and Patience, Mike's kids. Maybe especially to them. "Three visitors, actually," Andrew amended.

When Andrew paused, Brian prodded him along. He'd promised to stop by Lila's. Her oldest was on some special assignment and she hadn't heard from him in a week. She needed reassurance.

"And?"

Andrew gazed at him. Brian tried to remember when he'd seen so much sadness in his brother's eyes. "They were Mike's kids."

Was Andrew getting muddled? He knew the names and ages of not only his kids and their spouses and children but the names and ages of all his nieces, nephews and *their* spouses and children.

"Mike didn't have three kids," Brian reminded him. "He had two. Patrick and Patience."

Andrew's expression never changed. "Besides Patrick and Patience."

Brian's eyes narrowed and his mouth dropped open. "Mike had three other kids?" That didn't seem possible. They would have known, he and Andrew. "You're kidding, right?"

If anything, Andrew seemed more somber. "You know me better than that. I never kid about family."

"When? How?" Questions popped up in Brian's head like wild mushrooms after a summer rain. "Do they live in Aurora?"

An ironic smile twisted Andrew's lips. "Not only do they live in Aurora, but they're all cops, the lot of them."

"I'll take that seat now," Brian murmured, sinking down onto the barstool.

Chapter 4

Kasey dropped Zack off in a less than upscale part of town, in front of a motel. The area brought back memories of where she'd first stayed right after she'd staged her own death.

The idea to escape that had occurred to her the moment she'd come across an unclaimed Jane Doe who'd died at her hospital. It was almost like a sign telling her this was the way out. God forgive her, she'd managed to get the body out of the hospital's morgue in the wee hours of the night. She'd left it in the master bedroom of her house, taken care to dispose of the teeth so that a complete identification would be impossible. After taking a few possessions that were important to her, more for sentiment than for value, she'd torched the house where she and Jim had lived.

It killed her to do it, not just because she was leaving behind a life she'd struggled to make for herself, a life where she'd been truly happy, but because, to protect her grandmother, she had to die.

Six months later, she'd assumed that the furor over her death and the case had died down. Guessing that Jim's murderer felt more secure, and that she was no longer a threat, she'd mailed her grandmother a postcard with a carousel horse on it.

There'd been no message written on it, no return address and she had taken great pains to mail it a good fifty miles away from where she was actually staying. But she was fairly confident that her grandmother would make the connection and understand what the postcard implied. That she was still alive. Her grandmother had always loved carousels and had a small, precious collection of figurines depicting all sorts of different carousel horses. She'd given her grandmother several of the pieces herself, scraping together what money she could spare while wrestling with the staggering cost of putting herself through medical school.

As Zack got out of her car and shut the door, she realized today was her grandmother's birthday.

The ache in her chest came out of nowhere. With all her heart, Kasey wished she could at least pick up the phone to say happy birthday. But she couldn't risk it. For all she knew, the man she was running from, the man who had paid off the police detective to kill Jim and to try to kill her, might have even placed a tap on her grandmother's phone.

Anything was possible. And if he had, then all her plans, all these long, isolated months that saw her go from one place to another, afraid to even make eye contact, afraid to get close to anyone, would have been for nothing.

Zack leaned down to look into the car one last time. "Thanks again."

She brushed off his words and nodded at his side. "Get that looked at as soon as possible," she told him, shifting the vehicle into Reverse.

And then she took off.

He stood for a moment, watching her go down the street. Wondering what secrets she had. He would have bet his life she had more than her share.

But all that was for another time. Right now, he needed to check in, to let the captain know what had happened. After circling the multi-unit structure, he went toward the back. His room was on the second floor, facing the unpaved rear parking lot.

Zack tried to pull his thoughts together. He had to admit that he wasn't as clearheaded as he would have liked. Not because he was weak from the loss of blood, he was dealing with that. Without being vain, he prided himself on being pretty damn healthy and strong. No, his brain wasn't as focused as it normally was because the woman who had taken him in had really aroused his curiosity—among other things.

He wasn't quite sure what to make of it. Or her.

Letting himself into the rented room, he nearly saun-
tered right in, then thought to take an extra wide step
over the threshold so as not to disturb the flour he'd pur-
posely left there.

He went straight to the closet and pulled out another
shirt. Peeling off the one he had on, he glanced down
at the bandages. She'd been thorough all right,
wrapping them securely around his rib cage. His ribs
were sore where the other man had kicked him, but he
was pretty sure they weren't cracked. For one thing, it
didn't hurt to breathe. It was just sore. What did hurt
was the area where his wound was.

He was lucky to have found Kasey rather than
someone else who would have freaked out and left him
to bleed to death. Someday his luck was going to run
out. He just hoped it wouldn't happen for a few years
yet.

"Seales is dead," he was saying into his cell phone
less than ten minutes later. After changing, he'd made
a quick sweep of the area to make sure that nothing was
moved and that no one had entered via the window.
There were items he'd left seemingly scattered about,
items that he would have been able to tell if they'd been
moved even a fraction of an inch.

Nothing had been touched. And the thin layer of
flour along the threshold had been undisturbed. No one
had walked through it—although he almost had, he
thought with a rueful smile. That had been the first indication that Kasey Madigan had messed with his mind.

The deep, gravelly voice on the other end said, "Yeah, I know."

He should have known. Mike Valdez was always on top of everything. At times, he had a feeling the man didn't sleep, he just changed his batteries every so often. Valdez's dedication to the job had cost him two wives and a son.

"Woman walking her dog this morning discovered the body," the captain elaborated. "Nearly had a heart attack, they tell me. Didn't stop screaming until someone came over to see what was wrong. They called in Aurora's finest. So what happened?" Valdez asked.

"After the meeting broke up, I followed Seales to an Internet café. I think he's cheating—*was* cheating," Zack corrected himself since everything about the man was now in the past tense, "on his buddies. There were a few people in the café. I didn't think he saw me, but I guess he must have. When he slipped out the back, I did too. That was when he jumped me. He was waiting right at the door," Zack explained, irritated with himself for not being prepared. "Probably thought I was going to rat him out to Randall," he guessed, mentioning the name of the current leader of the identity-theft ring that he was dogging.

A roach ran over the toe of his boot as he talked. He stepped on it with his other foot, grinding it into nothingness. Spiders he didn't mind, but roaches were a different story. Roaches were filthy. He hated roaches.

"Why don't you present that to Randall?" Valdez suggested. Zack could almost hear the wheels in the man's head turning. "Tell him that your suspicions were aroused by Seales's actions and you were just following a hunch. Things got out of hand, he tried to kill you, you fought back."

Zack switched the phone to his other ear. He supposed it was worth a try. "You don't think my cover's been blown?"

"Only one way to find out," Valdez theorized. A chuckle followed his statement.

"Right," Zack sighed. He was going to march back into the lion's den—and hope the lion's already had lunch. "You know where to ship my body if something goes wrong, right?"

Valdez blew off the implication behind the words. He operated as if his men were invulnerable. "Hey, from what I hear, the Cavanaughs have always been damn lucky. Rumor has it that you're becoming one of them by proxy—real soon."

Since the wedding involved the chief of detectives, Zack was fairly certain that the topic was number one when it came to making the rounds at the precinct. "Nothing gets by you, does it, Captain?"

"Just my ex-wives' infidelities," the man cracked dryly. "Never saw either one coming until it was too late. By the way, the uniforms on the scene said there was a lot of blood behind the Internet café. Lab makes it out to be two different blood types." There was a pause, as if the man was waiting for him to say something. He didn't. "You get hurt, McIntyre?"

Zack looked down at his shirt. He still hadn't

buttoned it and the bandage around his rib cage was visible. "Nothing that won't heal."

"Keep it that way," Valdez ordered.

"I'll sure try, Captain." He knew that Valdez was about to go. His superior never talked more than was necessary. "By the way, the punk managed to slash my tires, when I couldn't begin to guess. I need a ride delivered to the motel."

"How did you get to the motel in the first place?"

He thought about Kasey, then decided Valdez didn't need to know about her. So he covered his butt by simply saying, "Hitched a ride with an angel."

"Never mind." Anticipating more, Valdez cut him off. "I don't think I want to know. Car'll be there soon," he promised, then abruptly broke the connection.

"Goodbye, Captain," Zack murmured sarcastically to the empty air. He flipped the phone closed and was about to put it away. Changing his mind, he flipped open the lid again. He hit a single button that would connect him to a preprogrammed number that represented the first phone number he'd ever memorized.

It barely rang once. A breathless "hello?" echoed in his ear.

He smiled to himself, picturing her as he said, "Hi, Mom."

"Zack! Zack, are you all right?" Lila McIntyre demanded, concern vibrating in every syllable.

Like his late father, his mother was part of the Aurora police force. Years ago, she'd been a detective, partnered with Brian Cavanaugh before a bullet had all but robbed her of the rest of her life. Brian had stopped the flow of blood with his own hand until the paramedics came and most likely saved her life.

She'd left the force after that to take care of him and his siblings. His father was responsible for that more than her wound was. He gave her no peace until she retired. And even then, he gave her no peace. It had been a hard life for his mother. For all of them.

You could take the woman out of the police force, but you couldn't take the police force out of the woman, Zack mused because once Frank was in high school, she'd come back to work. His father had insisted she take desk duty only and she'd reluctantly agreed, feeling that manning a desk was better than nothing.

During her years on the force, she became acquainted with all the bad things that life could throw at a person. Which made it twice as hard for her to watch not one or two but all four of her children go into law enforcement. As far back as he could remember, she was always a mother first and Detective McIntyre second.

He hated to make her worry, but at the same time, she understood his passion for the job. But that didn't mean she had to like it, she'd told him more than once, just before telling him how proud she was of him.

A lot of mixed signals in this family, Zack thought, not the least of which had been the relationship between his parents. His father, insecure and always feeling as if he had to live up to Brian Cavanaugh's image, became progressively abusive toward her. He'd lost count of the times he'd inserted himself between his parents to keep his mother safe. And all the while, there'd been a part of him that worried, worried that he was his father's son, that he'd inherited the gene that would make him into an unfit husband.

There was no reason to believe that would ever be put to the test. What woman would put up with the kind of life he led? he thought. He wasn't even going to attempt to find an answer to that. Which was why his relationships were always pleasant and short and the only intimacy that was ever allowed to occur was beneath the sheets, not between two souls.

That was okay, he had enough people in his life to love without that.

He tried to make his mother come around by kidding her. "No, Mom, I'm not all right. I'm being held prisoner by a bunch of roving gypsies. Starving roving gypsies," he amended. "They said they'll only let me go if you promise to make them one of your famous apple cinnamon pies."

"No problem. Shall I send it, or will they let you come and pick it up?" It was her way of asking when she would see him.

He thought for a moment. If everything went according to the plan, the noose would tighten around these so-called masterminds in the next couple of days. It all depended on whether or not he was a trusted member of the "team."

"I might be able to swing by on Sunday for a few minutes."

"Sunday." She tried to disguise it, but he heard the wistful note in her voice as she repeated the day. "Try to stay alive until then."

"I'll do my best, Mom." He knew that Brian Cavanaugh was one of the most decent men who'd ever walked the earth, but because in his heart he'd never stopped feeling like his mother's protector, he had to ask, "He treating you okay?"

"Like a princess, Zack."

"Not good enough, Mom," Zack said glibly. "I don't care if he is the chief of detectives, he should be treating you like a queen."

He heard his mother laugh lightly, like the girl she'd always been at heart. "Gives me something to look forward to, honey—besides seeing all my children's smiling faces. At the same time," she emphasized.

"If that's what you want, then you'd better find something to slip Frank. You know what a sourpuss he can be."

She laughed again and he caught himself thinking that it was a heartwarming sound. She laughed a lot more these days than she used to. "Funny, he says the same thing about you."

He had to get going. He hoped Valdez made good on his promise about the car. "Take care, Mom."

"I'm not the one running around in unsavory circles," she reminded him.

He knew she wanted to say something, to ask him not to volunteer for undercover work. But she didn't, which was what made her so great. "Point taken. I'll call you soon."

"I'll hold you to that," were her final words before she hung up.

Zack flipped the phone closed. As he stuck it back into his pocket, he thought he heard a car approaching. Crossing to the window, he looked out into the back parking lot.

And smiled. Good old Valdez. He always managed to come through.

Two days dragged by, feeding into one another like raindrops sliding down a windowpane. There was nothing to offset the two days and make them different.

Except that Kasey still found herself thinking about the man who had temporarily disrupted her life.

Zack.

Was that really his name, or had he just given her an alias? Two years ago, she would have never doubted anything anyone told her. Two years ago she had been incredibly naive for her age. Now she doubted everything, which made her jaded. Given a choice, Kasey would have preferred being that naive woman rather than this hardened person she had been forced to become. Not trusting anyone was so isolating. There were times she didn't think she could breathe.

But at least she was surviving, and for now, that was enough. Later she'd come up with a plan. Later, when she could gather her courage to her, she'd exact revenge for Jim and for herself, for the precious months she'd lost and for the life that had been taken from her the moment Jim died.

Standing on top of the ladder, she continued shifting books from one shelf to another, making room for the "new" arrivals that Edwin Owens, the shop owner, had managed to score from the last two estate sales he'd attended.

The shop was empty, which was more often than not the case. People frequented the quaint bookstore on weekends. During the week, they were lucky to see more than a couple of people a day. This was not a source of income for Edwin so much as a hobby. He loved old books and he had run out of space in his home. A secondhand bookstore seemed like the perfect solution.

As she worked, she let her mind wander. Because she sincerely doubted she would ever see the man again, she allowed her thoughts to go places that she'd kept off-limits these last eighteen months. She'd been operating like a robot, not a flesh-and-blood woman. It was easier that way.

Zack, she thought as she created a new space for yet another copy of *Walden,* had been exceeding good-looking. The kind of man women fantasized about—except for the bullet wound. But even that played into a fantasy, she realized. She leaned over precariously to one side, angling in a slim volume between two thicker ones. The fit was tight. Frowning, she moved the last book to the next shelf.

How many times did women conjure up scenarios where they nursed a wounded soldier back to health? It satisfied both the nurturer and the lover within each woman. Both of which had been leeched from her.

But she'd felt a certain amount of fulfillment, helping Zack. Ever since she was five and suddenly orphaned, she'd wanted to be a doctor. Even then she'd believed she could have saved her parents had she practiced medicine instead of watching them die before the paramedics arrived on the scene.

Right, saved them, she mocked herself. She hadn't even been able to save Jim. She hadn't even stayed to try. The second that police detective—the man who had been assigned to guard them and keep them safe in the hotel room—had opened fire on them, hitting Jim, she'd fled. Ducking out the door, she'd broken into a run and flew down the stairs.

She hadn't stopped running until she'd come to a Dumpster two blocks away. She'd hidden there, amid the waste and refuse. Praying that the stench would keep the killer from searching for her in there.

The stench had made her nauseous and dizzy, but she'd endured it for several hours, climbing out only when she thought it was safe. She'd learned about Jim's death via a news program blaring out onto the street from one of those appliance warehouses that kept more affordable items on the sidewalk. Up until that point, she'd been praying that he was alive.

She'd nearly passed out then. But somehow, she kept walking. Aware that people all around her were giving her strange looks. At that point, had the killer found her, she wouldn't have cared. Wouldn't have cared if she lived or died because Jim was gone.

But the will to survive was stronger than her heartbreak and eventually she forced herself to think—and to act.

Waiting until dark, she bided her time and slipped into the hospital where she'd worked via a back entrance that had momentarily been left unattended. Going to her locker, she'd gotten a change of clothes. She'd showered quickly in one of the stalls located on the maternity floor and then tried to figure out what to do next.

Eighteen months later, she was still trying to figure out what to do next, she mused. Maybe someday, she'd figure it out. Figure out what to do to put this life behind her.

The bell that hung over the doorway went off, signaling the entrance of a customer. Or, more likely, a browser.

Feeling vulnerable, perched on a ladder the way she was, Kasey turned around, intending on climbing down. But she'd moved too quickly, throwing the ladder's balance off. One moment she was standing on the top rung, the next moment, she was airborne. And heading for the floor.

Fast.

Chapter 5

The second he saw her fall, Zack ran into the shop and across the room. He made it from the doorway to the ladder in less than half a heartbeat, managing to catch Kasey just before she hit the floor.

The wound in his side complained bitterly at the strain of her weight, compounded by velocity. He figured it was a small price to pay. At the very least, he owed her one for what she'd done the other night.

"Gotcha!"

The triumphant word whooshed out of his mouth as he pulled her against him in order to keep his balance. Her hand instantly splayed against his chest. Zack was *not* prepared for the force of the electricity that came charging at him out of nowhere. It took effort to maintain his equilibrium.

For a split second, the air went rushing out of her lungs, squeezed out as she landed squarely in his arms. God, but they felt strong. And muscular.

Somewhere in the back of her mind, she couldn't help thinking that it couldn't have gone better if they'd rehearsed this.

At the same time, she became aware of something very intense happening all along her nerve endings. Mentally, she scrambled to collect herself.

"How did you find me?" she asked.

"I saw a paper bag in your place with the logo Rare Treasures. You said you worked in a bookstore. I took a chance. It paid off."

"You took a bigger chance," she pointed out. "You could have broken your stitches catching me."

He looked directly into her eyes, further unsettling her. "You could have broken something else if I'd let you land on the floor," he pointed out.

"No argument," she conceded. "How's the wound coming along?" she asked.

"It's healing."

It struck her as odd that he made no effort to release her. She wasn't exactly weightless. "I think you can put me down now."

"Yes, I know." Even so, he allowed himself one last moment to savor the sensation of holding her. He couldn't have explained why, but having her in his arms felt right. Zack could only speculate that his covert life had taken its toll.

He did enjoy the company of beautiful women, a rarity when he was on the job.

Setting her down, Zack stepped back, then fired off a rhetorical question. "Don't you know you're not supposed to stand on the top rung of a ladder? You could have taken a really nasty spill if I hadn't come in just when I did."

"If you hadn't come in when you did, I wouldn't have turned so fast and lost my balance," she countered. "And there would have been no reason to play the knight in shining armor." Or faded denim, she added silently. "What are you doing here, anyway?"

He grinned. "Besides catching you?"

Something in the pit of her stomach reacted to his grin. She didn't like it. She stepped back, bumping up against the ladder.

Stilling it before it fell over, she did what she could to recapture her dignity. Kasey raised her chin defiantly. "Yes, besides that."

He was well aware that he was in her space and made no effort to back off. It'd been a while now since he'd felt human. Since he'd felt like a red-blooded man. She made him remember that. "I thought I owed you more than just a thank-you for what you did."

Kasey shrugged his words away. The last thing she wanted was to get involved with someone on *any* level. "You don't owe me anything."

"I come from a very large family that believes in paying their dues and their debts."

She moved by him, turning her attention to the books in the cart she had yet to alphabetize before shelving them. "You're making too much out of it."

He followed her, entertained by the way her hips moved when she walked. "Well, my life might not seem like that much to you," he allowed, "but it's the only one I have—"

She spared him a glance. Why wasn't he going away? "I didn't mean to imply that your life isn't important, it's just that my part in it is negligible. If I hadn't taken you in, someone else would have."

He sincerely doubted that. "I knocked on several doors that night. No one opened theirs." Glancing down at the books, he moved one ahead of several others. "Except you."

"I didn't open the door," she reminded him. "I was coming home and found you splayed across my doorstep. Makes a difference." She blew out a breath. Ordinarily, it wasn't this difficult getting people to go away and leave her alone. "If it makes you feel better, I absolve you of all debts that you think you owe me."

He smiled, offering her another book. "Goes there," he pointed to the space. Then he shook his head. "It doesn't work that way," he clarified when she eyed him quizzically.

"Oh?" Lowering her eyes, she went back to alphabetizing—and to ignoring him. The latter effort was completely unsuccessful. "And how does it work?"

He gave her his game plan. "I take you out for some

coffee. If you find yourself having not that terrible a time, then we go on to dinner at some future date."

Her head jerked up. "Date?"

"Strictly in the calendar sense," he assured her, at the same time wondering what could have spooked her this way. He had his suspicions on that matter. "Not in the male-female sense—although, arguably," he allowed, "there will be one of each present at the table."

She looked at him for a long moment. The man certainly wasn't at a loss for words. Or twists and turns. "Are you a disbarred lawyer?"

The question tickled him even though he had little use for lawyers. He saw them as the enemy, getting people off on a technicality, scum he or one of the other detectives had busted their butt to capture. "Why disbarred?"

She glanced down at his attire. "Because I never knew any practicing lawyer who walked around in torn jeans."

Zack crossed his arms before him, his amusement growing. "So you figure I must have done something dishonorable and gotten tarred and feathered by my own kind?"

She shrugged carelessly, squatting down to take inventory. "Something like that."

"Well, I'm not a lawyer, past or present. What I am is thirsty." He scanned the store, listening for a sound, an indication that someone else was in the store, someone who could cover for her for a few minutes. "When do you get your break?"

"I don't," she informed him crisply. "I'm the only

one in the store so I can't just leave on a whim." She hoped that was enough to make him back off and leave.

She should have known better.

"Slavery was outlawed, you know." He had this uncontrollable urge to wind a strand of her hair around his forefinger just to feel if it was as silky as it looked.

She resented his implication. She actually liked working here. It was quiet, and she liked old books. "I get an hour lunch. I lock up the store from twelve to one."

It was ten now. He had to be on his way by eleven-thirty. That taken into account, her time frame didn't work for him.

"Can't you push it up just this once?" He gestured about the empty store. "I'm guessing you won't get an argument from the throngs."

She stopped looking through the books and rose to her feet. Zack made her uneasy, and yet, he stimulated her.

She didn't need this kind of trouble. And yet...

She took a breath, knowing she was going to regret her next move. "Look, if you really want coffee, I keep a pot on in the back. It's Edwin's small way of competing with the bookstores that have cafés built into them." There was a specified tiny area for the customer to sit, but no books could go near the coffee. They were sacred to Edwin. He would sacrifice a customer before he sacrificed a book.

Zack didn't want her going through any extra work. "I don't really want coffee," he confessed. "I want an excuse to spend some time with you."

After having it as her constant and only companion

for the last eighteen months, she couldn't just divorce herself from suspicion. "Why?"

He usually didn't get this much resistance when he expressed interest in a woman. "Why do you need to have everything spelled out?" he asked, amused. "It takes all the fun out of the surprises that life springs on you."

He saw her stiffen slightly and knew he'd said the wrong thing, but what part of it was wrong he hadn't a clue. She was like a puzzle. An intriguing, beautiful, blue-eyed puzzle.

She moved back, away from him and wound up hitting the cart, hard. Books flew off the cart, spilling onto the floor.

Swallowing a choice swear word, Kasey dropped to her knees and started gathering the books together. She'd alphabetize them later.

"I don't like surprises," she told him through clenched teeth.

Zack knelt down beside her, picking up several books at a time and sliding them back onto the cart.

"Oh, but you should." He reached over for several books that had spilled out by her side. Picking them up, he straightened only to accidentally brush up against her. Again, electricity hummed through his veins. His eyes held hers for a long moment, temptation swirling through him.

"Some of the nicest things happen that way," he went on to say, his voice low.

Kasey felt as if she'd been zapped by a low-voltage Taser. Damn, what was the matter with her? Where was this pull coming from? She'd never been one of those people who slipped easily from relationship to relationship. Jim had been only the second man she'd ever slept with and that was only after she'd given her heart to him. This man was a complete stranger to her. So why was her body suddenly on high alert? What was this wild, damp palm feeling, and where was it coming from?

For that matter, where had the air in her lungs gone? She couldn't breathe, as if he'd stolen her supply of oxygen.

"I don't like surprises," she repeated, her voice hardly above a whisper.

"I do," he told her, one word slowly following the last. "Sometimes."

And this, he thought, this sexual pull that was drawing him to her, was certainly one of the nicer surprises he'd encountered in quite some time.

The next moment, the books were forgotten, abandoned on the floor where they'd fallen. Instead, he drove his fingers into her hair, tilted her head back and kissed her with all the feeling erupting within him.

She didn't disappoint him.

Lightning flashed as a sweetness spilled out through his veins. One taste of honey led to another and then another. He deepened the kiss, for a single second allowing himself to forget the life-and-death situation he was currently in, to forget that he consistently placed his life on the line and could be, at any moment, wiped away from the face of the earth without a trace.

Right now, nothing else mattered but this woman and her incredibly sweet, exciting mouth.

He wanted more.

More from her, more from himself.

Don't let's get carried away, he silently chided. He was supposed to have more control over himself than this. Okay, so she was damn beautiful and he was really attracted to her, but he was made of sterner stuff than that, right? He couldn't allow this to make him rejuggle his priorities. He was on an assignment for God's sake. Dedication had his job coming before pleasure—even if, right at this moment, he didn't want it to.

Just another second, he bartered with himself, kissing her harder.

Oh God, what was going on here? Why was she letting this happen? Letting? She was right there in it, absorbing and relishing. And reciprocating. But this wasn't the woman she'd become in these last eighteen months. Kasey Madigan shied away from any kind of physical contact, certainly away from something as intimate as a kiss. Because that's what it was, intimate. Not pleasant, not fleeting, not friendly. Intimate. With a capital *I*.

His kiss slammed into her, going right through all the layers she'd wound so tightly around herself and aimed itself straight for where she lived.

Straight for her inner core. Her heart, which was beating wildly, was in danger of wearing itself out.

Summoning all her willpower, Kasey pulled back. As she did so, she realized that her breath came in small, shaky gasps. Her eyes on his, she squared her shoulders and did what she could to appear unfazed. Even so, she sincerely doubted anyone was that good an actor.

Still, she tried to sound unaffected. She would have been more convincing if she didn't sound so breathless, Kasey thought ruefully. Hoping that he wouldn't notice she was just playing a fool's game.

"Was that to illustrate a point?" she finally asked him.

For a moment, he just looked at her, as if her words weren't making any sense. "If it was, I lost the thread," he confessed.

She felt flustered inside. It was a long, downhill slide from the confident surgeon she'd been such a short while ago. Needing something to do with her hands, to keep busy, she began to place the books back up on the cart. Alphabetizing was out of the question. She would have needed to know the alphabet for that.

"You shouldn't have done that," Kasey murmured.

He wasn't sure if she was addressing the words to him, or to herself. In either case, his reaction was the same. "I think we're going to have our first disagreement, Kasey."

Summoning indignation, a surefire male repellant, she eyed him sharply. But the smile on his lips was so disarming, she had trouble maintaining her annoyance—or any semblance of it. She did, however, want him to know something. "I don't do casual."

He did. It was the only thing he did. Because of his background, of who he was, he didn't do serious, or commitment.

But what just happened didn't fit his normal criteria. "There was nothing casual about that kiss, Kasey. Not on either end," he added. She was going to ask him to leave, he could feel it. And in reality, he supposed he should be going. But he wanted to leave the door open between them. "Does this mean I don't get any coffee?"

She stopped stacking books and looked at him intently. Things didn't "just happen" in her life. Not anymore. She didn't allow them to.

"Why are you here?" she asked.

"I already told you. I'm in your debt and I just want to repay you by taking you out to dinner, but I had a feeling that you're not exactly the trusting kind, so I figured we could start out by going out or in—" he nodded toward the small table in the back where the coffeemaker stood "—*for coffee.* Baby steps."

She pressed her lips together. She could still taste his on them. It sent a small, thrilling ripple through her. "*That* was not a baby step."

He inclined his head, as if in agreement. "I'll do better next time."

Kasey didn't know whether to feel unnerved—or thrilled. "Just what makes you think that there'll be a next time?"

"What makes you think there won't?" he countered, his eyes holding her prisoner.

The sound of the bell announcing someone's entrance into the store interrupted them.

He thought he saw something akin to fear flicker in her eyes as she quickly turned her head to see who had entered. What was it that she was anticipating? More to the point, what was she afraid of? For one fleeting moment, Kasey hadn't looked like a clerk about to wait on a customer but like someone expecting something— or someone—far worse.

Glancing toward the door, Zack saw an older, well-dressed woman walk into the shop. She had the look of old money and eccentricity about her. Probably someone wanting a first edition or a hidden treasure amid the discarded and neglected tomes. As for him, the only hidden treasure he saw was the woman with wariness in her eyes.

Damn, but this job had to be getting to him. He didn't usually wax poetic this way.

Maybe it was a good thing they'd been interrupted. He was letting himself get carried away when he knew he shouldn't. He needed a clear head, to be on his toes, in order to carry off his ruse. One false move and he was done for. The wound in his side was a reminder of that.

Backing away, he said, "I'll leave you to your customer." And then added just before he slipped out, "But I'll be back."

As she smiled warmly at the woman who'd entered the shop, Kasey glanced over toward the door. She watched Zack go, not knowing if she should be thinking of leaving the area again, or if she'd just been given a reason to put down roots.

Not able to deal with the internal debate, Kasey turned back toward the woman in the shop and said in her friendliest voice, "May I help you?"

* * *

Only when he was several blocks away did Zack remove the book from his jacket and place it carefully into his pocket. The book had fallen off the cart onto the floor. One of the books that he knew Kasey had handled. At the very first opportunity, he would take it down to the APD lab. The tech there, Jeremy, owed him a favor and he was about to call it in. He wanted to lift a set of her prints from either the front or back cover.

The inherent uneasiness he detected from her had him wondering. Was Kasey some kind of fugitive? Either from the law, or from something else? Was she in trouble?

The first step toward unraveling the mystery was finding out if her prints were on file, either in the crime database or one of the armed services. Maybe she was an enlistee who'd had enough and had gone AWOL.

Or, even more possibly, she was running away from an abusive husband or lover.

He hadn't seen any bruises on her, but there were many ways to bruise a woman without leaving behind telltale physical marks.

His father had been an expert at that, he couldn't help thinking. He clenched his hands into fists as he walked. Ben McIntyre had slashed away at his wife with a brutal tongue that was as hurtful, as damaging in its own way as a cat-o'-nine-tails.

There was no point to this, to remembering a past he couldn't change. With determination, Zack shook off the specter of his father. He didn't like to think about him, or dwell on the fact that they were related.

Besides, he could be jumping the gun. There could be some other, totally unrelated reason why Kasey seemed to be giving off an aura of suspicion.

For now, though, he needed to get to a loft over on the other side of town. So far, Randall didn't give the impression that he suspected anything was amiss. Randall had believed his story. He seemed almost relieved to be rid of Seales, referring to the hacker as a punk, a wiseass and a liability. Randall was more than willing to believe him when he said that he had offed Seales when he'd discovered that the underling was trying to branch out on his own and, ironically, steal some of the identities that the group had already taken. He'd gotten rid of the loose cannon, Zack had said. And Randall had believed him.

Megalomaniacs tended to believe that the world centered around them and that everyone else knew it. That was often what ultimately tripped them up.

Zack was counting on it.

Chapter 6

As she approached her development three nights later, Kasey noticed how tightly she held the steering wheel. Taking a deep breath, she slowly released her grip.

She was getting carried away, letting her mind go to places where it didn't belong right now. Letting herself yearn for things she wasn't supposed to think about, not for a long, long time.

But that was because of the couple.

Just before she'd locked up, she'd discovered a couple in the back of the shop. They'd been there earlier and had made two separate purchases, each buying a book of poetry that could have easily made someone's list of classics. Checking to make sure that the shop was empty, she'd found them reading to one another in soft, modulated voices. She didn't think things like that happened anymore, not in a world that was so fast-paced, so electronically oriented. Reading out loud to one another seemed so beautifully old-fashioned. One human being reaching out to another.

Oh God, she missed that more than she could say. She missed being part of something larger than herself.

She'd been doing this for eighteen months now and in many ways, she still wasn't used to being relegated to the sidelines, to the life of someone standing on the outside, looking in, like a starving guest barred from the banquet.

She still wasn't used to always being alert, always being on her guard, ready to pick up and go at a moment's notice because of something she perceived to be a threat—even when it might not be.

She didn't even know, hadn't known the other two times she'd taken her belongings and vanished in the night, if it was actually necessary to go. Maybe she hadn't needed to go after she'd settled down the first time. Maybe the florist where she'd gotten a job was only taking an interest in her because he was attracted to her, or liked to talk, or was being nosy. Or any one of a number of reasons that had nothing to do with who she was. Or had been.

Maybe it was just her paranoia that made her flee and not any actual threat to her person. More than anything, she wanted to believe that the man who had ordered Jim's murder was no longer looking for her. Was satisfied that she'd died in that fire.

Because in a way she had.

Kasey pulled her car up outside the garage as had gotten to be her habit. There were times when she felt as if her old life, the life of a surgeon, the life as Jim's fiancée, had all been just a dream. Or something that had happened to someone else she'd only read about.

Lately it felt as if she'd always been running. As if she'd always been suspicious of a lingering glance, of people who turned in her direction for a second look. Because she was ready to run at a moment's notice, nothing was permanent in her life and she'd been someone who'd always longed for permanence with every fiber of her being. Longed for it ever since her parents had been killed.

Now, she rented spaces in which to perch until the next getaway.

God, but she was tired of it.

Wasn't it time to stop? To settle down and start again? She'd changed her hair color, her name, her vocation, couldn't she just go on pretending to be Kasey Madigan and forge a life that would suit her? That wasn't asking very much, was it? To have a little stability? To stop feeling as if she was living out of a suitcase? She wanted to buy, not just rent. She wanted a bed of her own, not one that came with a furnished house or room. It offended her sense of order and interfered with who and what she'd once longed to be.

Kasey closed her eyes, drawing her hand through her hair, as if to untangle her thoughts, her feelings. This restlessness wasn't helping her cause any.

Damn it, she knew what was wrong with her, she

thought, opening her eyes again. It was that kiss, that man who'd scrambled her very brain, upheaving everything she'd struggled to set in place. Safeguards she needed in order to continue this bland life that she had to lead right now. The longings existed, all right, but she'd managed to keep them under wraps.

Until Zack had come along.

Why was she even thinking about him? She hadn't seen him since he walked out of the shop three days ago. Most likely, she'd never see him again.

It was that couple that had started her thinking. Started her dreaming…

So why wasn't it Jim she was dreaming of, instead of some stranger.

She was just tired, that's all, Kasey told herself. Tired and weary of all the pretending. But it was all for her own good. It had kept her alive all these months.

To what end? she challenged herself. She couldn't enjoy herself, couldn't do anything like a normal woman. Because she couldn't put her guard down in case they were still looking for her.

Kasey blew out a breath, frustrated. If she lived like this any longer, he'd win, that man who wanted her dead. Carmine Pasquale would win because he'd have made her afraid to live her life and afraid to be herself. So what was the point of living at all?

Okay, Kasey decided suddenly, making up her mind, she refused to be cowed any longer. If Zack ever showed up again, she wasn't going to try to push him away. Instead, she'd act on her instincts—if she hadn't buried them completely or lost them for lack of use, she amended with a silent laugh.

Feeling ever so slightly better, Kasey got out of the car.

And nearly swallowed her tongue in an effort not to scream.

A figure stepped out of the shadows directly by the little house she was renting.

Zack.

Stifling a scream, Kasey took in a deep breath to steady her suddenly frayed nerves. That was twice in one week the man had surprised her. Three times if she counted their first encounter.

Pushing her heart out of her throat, angry at being rattled, Kasey demanded, "What are you doing here?"

"Waiting for you."

Zack had put in his time in his other identity, and found a way to report in with the information to Valdez that something big was going down in the next couple of days. For now, there was downtime and he'd decided to use his to drop in on Kasey. Except that she wasn't home yet. Ordinarily, he would have shrugged his shoulders and left.

Except that he didn't. Not finding her home yet just made him want to see her even more. So he'd decided to pick up a couple of containers of coffee and wait for her. He'd all but given up, thinking that she'd gone somewhere overnight, when he saw her car turning down the street.

"I brought my own coffee this time," he volunteered,

indicating the containers in his hands, "and yours. It's kind of cool, though, because I've been here a while. If you have a microwave, you could warm it up and have it the way you like."

It sounded so incredibly sweet—and normal. Except normal and sweet weren't part of her world anymore.

"Why are you doing all this?" She wanted him to give her an answer she could cling to, an answer that made sense. Like maybe he was here for no other reason than because he wanted to see her. But even so, suspicions began eating away at her, telling her to be on her guard.

No matter how much she wanted to turn a deaf ear to the warning voice in her head, she couldn't do it, couldn't just ignore it. Couldn't just turn over a whole new leaf, walk down a different road.

Why not? You did the night Jim was killed. The night you decided to go on the run and faked your own death.

She had no answer.

"I just wanted to talk to you," he told her. "Can we go to your house?" he asked and nodded at the back of the small white brick building facing the alley.

These last eighteen months, she'd made it a point not to stay outside a second longer than she absolutely had to. She felt like a target that way.

But what if she was bringing the enemy into her house?

Idiot, you've already brought him there once and he didn't kill you, did he? So maybe he's harmless.

And maybe Zack was biding his time for some reason.

So she shrugged in response to his question. "It's a nice night. Why don't we just stay out and look at the stars?"

He glanced up at the black sky. "You see stars?" he asked in moderate surprise. "You've got better vision than I do, Kasey. I don't see any."

That was because there weren't any, she realized, looking up. She'd just assumed that there would be. So much for heavenly backup, she thought sarcastically. "I thought I saw..." Kasey's voice trailed off helplessly.

He saw through the excuse, or thought he did. "You don't have to be afraid of me, Kasey. I'm harmless." He grinned. "You can ask my sisters."

Leaning against the side of her car, she finally accepted the coffee container he'd offered her. The logo on the side boasted a large coffeehouse chain. That meant he'd picked them up at the strip mall on the outskirts of the development. She'd noticed it on her way home, but never stopped to get any. All she'd ever wanted to do was just get home in one piece and lock the door behind her.

After removing the lid, she took a sip. It was still relatively warm. She tried to tell herself that it was the coffee, not his grin that wove its way through her system, warming everything in its path.

"You have sisters?" She realized there was a hint of longing in her voice.

He nodded. "Two. And a brother," he added. "But Frank's testimony might not be too flattering. I used to order him around a lot when he was little."

She could almost visualize him doing it. "When did that stop?"

Zack lowered his coffee container and glanced at his watch. "Best guess, sometime next month. Maybe the month after that."

Zack saw the corners of her mouth curve slightly. Definitely a sight worth waiting for, he thought.

"I wish I had siblings."

She looked more surprised than he did at the admission. He had a feeling she hadn't meant to say that. Hadn't meant to give him any kind of insight into her life. Why?

"You're an only child?"

It wasn't so much of a question as a subtle prod to get her to open up about herself. However little that might be, it was better than nothing. Jeremy had had the book he'd lifted from the bookstore for three days now. But the overworked lab tech hadn't gotten a chance to run the prints for him, or even determine if there was a viable set available. There'd been a ten-car pileup on the interstate around the time he'd given Jeremy the book. The need to determine which of the cars was initially at fault took precedence over a personal favor, even if he'd couched it in nebulous language which indicated that the person might have something to do with his ongoing case.

There were almost too many pieces of evidence to count in the pileup case. That meant Jeremy wouldn't be at his disposal for at least several more days.

So, in his downtime, Zack'd decided to fall back on old-fashioned methods: getting the person to talk about themselves.

Except that in this case, the lady was a little more

closemouthed than the average drop-dead gorgeous female. A lot more, actually, he amended.

Still, the woman was very easy on the eyes and this wasn't exactly a hardship for him, especially since being around her contrasted so drastically with the dregs of society that he dealt with the rest of the day. Though he gave no indication, there were times it dragged him down. As did pretending to be one of the parasites who lived off the labor of others, which was the way he viewed any sort of thief, especially the ones who specialized in identity theft, messing with a person's life and undoing years of hard work and effort in the blink of an eye and the stroke of a key.

He was really looking forward to getting the goods on these particular bastards and winding up the case. But right now, he wanted to spend a little quality time with a very beautiful lady.

Kasey heard the curiosity in his voice. Her pulse rate instantly spiked, even though she told herself that his curiosity was just the garden-variety kind. She took a breath, willing herself to steady her erratic pulse. There was nothing amiss here, she was reading too much into it. What harm would it do to admit a small part of the truth to this man, to tell him about her family structure? After all, it wasn't as if she was dropping bread crumbs that would lead him to her actual identity. A great many people out there had no siblings. She was just one of a crowd.

Which was exactly the way it needed to be for the time being.

"Yes," she replied, "I am. When I was growing up, I

always wondered what it would have been like to have a brother or sister."

He allowed himself a smile as he thought of his own adolescent years. "Chaotic comes to mind," he admitted, leaning against the car beside her.

Zack would have much rather gone inside her house, but for now, he didn't want to push it. He had a feeling that if he did, she'd make up some quick excuse and go inside—alone. He needed to earn her trust. Nothing he hadn't done many times before with other, far more lethal people.

"When we were growing up, there was always fighting." At least, when his father wasn't around. When Ben McIntyre was in the house, they walked on egg-shells, mainly because they didn't want their mother getting the brunt of the verbal abuse. "No bloodshed— except once," he amended, remembering.

Her eyes widened just a touch. "Bloodshed? What happened?"

He paused for a moment, getting the facts organized in his head. "Frank grabbed Riley's snow globe that some guy had given her a couple years back and took off, taunting her. Riley tackled him. He went down, breaking the globe and cutting his forehead. Mom rushed him to the hospital. Frank needed five stitches."

"What did Riley need?"

"A pillow to sit down on for the next couple of days." He frowned, remembering how helpless he'd felt. Corporal punishment was a great deal more common when he was growing up, but he'd still felt it was wrong, that there had to be another way to handle things other than hitting someone half your size. He'd tried to stop his father that night, tried to protect Riley. And had gotten beaten himself for his trouble. "My father was a firm believer in corporal punishment if he thought the situation warranted it."

Her grandmother resorted to the silent treatment the one or two times the woman had wanted her to bear the consequences of her behavior. It was enough to make her rethink her actions. She'd grown up healthy and happy. She wouldn't have traded her childhood for Zack's even though he had siblings.

"Your father sounds like a stern man."

"He wasn't an easy man to get along with."

"Wasn't," Kasey repeated, waiting for him to fill in the details for her.

"He died," Zack told her matter-of-factly, not adding that as far as the family was concerned, Ben McIntyre had died not once, but twice. The first time was when his father had arranged circumstances to appear as if he'd been executed while on the job as, ironically, an undercover vice cop. The second and last time had been when his mother had shot him to keep his father from killing Brian Cavanaugh. The chief of detectives had tried to stop him from making off with the money he'd stolen. The money he'd hidden in the house five years earlier and was trying to dig up so that he could go live with his mistress.

That was the kind of story he kept to himself. Enough people had read the news in the paper when it had all gone down. He had needed some time to get over the events and put them behind him. The specter of his father loomed large for more than one reason. He was currently trying to move on with his life. As were the other members of his family.

"I'm sorry." He heard the compassion in her voice as she touched his arm. Touched his soul.

Zack shrugged, not at her compassion, but at the way his father's death had affected him and his siblings. "As far as I'm concerned, he died a long time ago."

Kasey shook her head, confused. "I don't understand."

That wasn't her fault. He'd left out a large part of the narrative. The part that bothered him most, he supposed. "He was a different man years ago. I think the job got to him, changed him. Made him into somebody who was quick to anger. Someone devoid of sympathy. And it was hardest on my mother."

He loved his mother, she thought. That spoke well for him. "What job would that be?" Jim had had a similar complaint about his own father. Before suffering a fatal heart attack, the man had been a much-sought-after civil lawyer, the kind who forgot about promises made to his young son. Forgot dates that were important to members of his family. Had Zack's father been a lawyer? That gave him something in common with Jim and in an odd way, drew her closer to him.

Zack shook his head. He'd already said too much. "Doesn't matter. He's gone now." Mustering a smile, he nodded at the container in her hands. "So how do you like cold coffee?"

She took another sip before answering, as if to back up her words.

"Not bad, actually." The longer she stayed with him, the more she wanted to. She needed to leave while she still could. "Listen, I don't mean to be rude, but I really am very tired."

He could see why. "They do have you keeping horrible hours."

Edwin was good to her and she didn't want Zack getting the wrong idea about the older man. "That's just until the owner gets back. There's been a death in his family and he had to fly back East to make funeral arrangements. I told him to take his time and I'd hold down the fort. Usually, I work just the morning or the afternoon shift, not both."

He liked the way moonlight caressed her skin, making it almost translucent. "He's lucky to have someone as dedicated as you."

"It works both ways," she replied with a vague shrug of her shoulders as she looked away.

The way she saw it, she was lucky to have gotten the job. Edwin hadn't asked her any long, tedious questions during her interview. It was as if the man sensed her situation and was kind enough not to press the subject. Before she'd gotten her job at the bookstore, she'd gone to several other places whose ads she'd found in the paper. They had all turned her down for one reason or another. Mainly, she was certain, because she had no list of references, no contact numbers to call. Saying she was new in town wasn't enough. Her potential employers wanted to know about her last job, her last address. The next time she moved on, she was going to find a way to fabricate not just a driver's license, but references and previous employers, as well.

The next time.

The thought of having to go through all that again was oppressive and not something she wanted to deal with right now.

Kasey straightened, holding out the empty container as she flashed a quick smile. "Thank you for the coffee."

She was leaving, he thought. And he didn't want her to go.

Chapter 7

"I'd like to come in."

She looked at Zack for a long, endless moment, not knowing what to say. It wasn't that she didn't want him to come in. She did, and that was the problem. She wanted him to come in and all that the simple action implied.

Definitely not smart.

But then, she wasn't feeling very smart right now. Just vulnerable. And maybe a little bit needy, as well. A very bad combination and she knew it even if she couldn't seem to block it the way that she normally did.

The best she could do was hope that he would back away. "I don't think that would be a very good idea, Zack."

Probably not, he thought. But then again, he had a feeling she was worth the risk. And if this didn't go anywhere, she'd be out of his system. Either way, he needed to move forward.

Ever so lightly, he slid a forefinger down along her cheek, his eyes never leaving hers.

"I won't do anything you don't want me to," he promised. "I just want to talk, to connect for a half an hour or so."

He'd be connecting with someone who didn't really exist, who wasn't there. But, oh God, she ached to be there, to be herself if only just for a little while. To remember what it was like to feel something other than leery. Still, it was hard going against habits she'd taken up to ensure her own self-preservation.

"It's late," she pointed out. God, did that sound as lame to him as it did to her?

Kasey was weakening, he could hear it in her voice. He pressed his advantage. He had no idea why this was suddenly so important to him, but it was. Maybe, in the middle of all these people out to cheat and steal, he needed to be with someone decent for more than a fleeting second.

Zack supposed he could just drive home to his mother's house. His mother, bless her, would always welcome him with open arms. It didn't matter what time of night or day, she was there for him, for his brother and for his sisters. But she was finally forming a new life for herself, and, like as not, Brian was probably there at the house, as well. As much as he was glad for both of them—and he did like Brian Cavanaugh—he wasn't sure if he actually wanted the image of rousing his mother and Brian out of the same bed vividly imprinted in his head. She was, after all, his mother and mothers and sex were not to be thought of in the same sentence. It just didn't seem right.

Which meant the woman before him had to restore his faith in humanity. Zack rather liked that option.

"I won't stay long," he promised.

Kasey sighed. She pretended she was actually fighting this, even though on some level she already knew how all this was going to turn out.

"You're not going to take no for an answer, are you?" It was a rhetorical question.

Zack's answer surprised her. "I will if you want me to."

Kasey pressed her lips together. Had he said "no," she would have summoned the resolve to leave him leaning against her vehicle and gone inside, locking the door behind her. But Zack had placed her needs before his. That completely blew up the last shred of her resolve.

He probably knew it, too, she thought, looking up at his chiseled profile.

The man was good. Very, very good. And undoubtedly wanted to be bad. Very, very bad.

"C'mon," she murmured. She nodded her head toward her house, indicating that he should follow her.

Kasey led the few steps that it took to reach her back door. Taking out her key, she unlocked it and reached inside to turn on the light. Instantly, everything was bathed with enough illumination to seriously rival sunlight.

Zack blinked, then squinted in order not to be overcome with the amount of brightness everywhere. The contrast between moonlight and this was startlingly dramatic. It took a few seconds for his eyes to adjust. "You've changed the lighting since I was here last."

Kasey smiled, shaking her head as she closed the door behind him.

"You didn't see the house in the evening," she reminded him. "You came to just at dawn. The sun was rising. There was no need for lights then."

He thought for a second and realized she was right. Everything was still rather blurry from that night. "Why do you have it so bright?" he asked. The preponderance of her furnishings, he also realized, were white, as well. It was like being caught in a snowstorm.

"I don't like the dark," she answered simply.

There was a great deal more to it than that, but she saw no reason to elaborate. When the lights were set at maximum illumination, there was absolutely no place for anyone to hide, no shadows to use for cover. Everything was out in the open. As it should be. If someone was in here, she wanted to be aware the second she opened the door, *not* the minute she walked into a room. A minute could prove fatal.

As it had for Jim.

Zack glanced around her shoulder at the wall. There was a dimmer, not a switch there. That meant that they didn't have to go blind. "Do you mind if I turn it down a bit?" His hand hovered over the dimmer. "A few notches below the aurora borealis?"

Kasey glanced around the house one more time. There was no one here but them. Taking the empty coffee containers from him, she crossed to the kitchen to throw them out.

"Knock yourself out," she tossed over her shoulder.

The lighting changed instantly from supernova-bright to seductively intimate. Somewhere in her soul, she knew that was going to happen, knew it the moment she'd said he could come inside. Even so, for just a split second, she stopped walking, then resumed again, a fluttery, nervous feeling buzzing all around inside of her. She knew she was on the cusp of something she couldn't control.

And yet, she didn't want to back away.

Kasey was exceedingly aware of her every movement, her every gesture. She could all but feel her breath in her lungs as she turned around again.

"Trying to save on electricity for me?" she quipped.

"Never a bad thing in California," he countered. "Turning down those million-watt strobes might just save us all from experiencing another county-wide brownout."

She crossed back from the garbage, after depositing the containers. "Very ecology-minded of you," she commented drolly.

"We all need to do our share." Zack said the words so seriously, she couldn't decide if he was just bantering, or if he meant what he said.

Most likely not, she decided. Men usually had simpler goals in mind. "It's also more intimate that way," she went on to point out.

He grinned. It was hard to explain why the spreading of his lips and a glimpse of his teeth undid her so, but it did, going straight to her gut like a classic boxer's one-two punch.

"That, too," he agreed. His eyes were already caressing her. Undressing her. Excitement thundered through her veins. "Nice little bonus for doing a good deed."

She could hardly catch her breath—and he hadn't even done anything yet. Except make her want him.

Badly.

"I'm not a one-night stand, Zack," she told him softly. She needed him to know.

The grin faded. "I know that."

Platitudes, he was giving her platitudes, she told herself, fiercely trying to do whatever she could to keep from sliding down the slippery slope that had just opened up before her. And enticingly beckoned to her. He'd say anything to get her into bed. That's what men did. So why didn't that incense her? Why was she still standing there like some love-struck adolescent, crazy-glued in place?

"How would you know that?" she challenged. "You don't know anything about me."

"Some things you just know," he told her, slipping his hands around her waist.

It wasn't a line, it was the truth. He sensed things about her, things he had no way of knowing right now. Except that he did.

Drawing her closer, Zack hungrily lowered his mouth to hers.

Half of him was prepared to have her pull away, knowing that if she did, he wouldn't pursue it any further, even though he wanted to. Wanted to badly.

It would be a struggle resisting, but he refused to be like his father, to put his own needs and demands above the woman he was with. But Kasey didn't back away. She didn't wedge her hands between them, didn't push against his chest in an effort to separate them. If anything, she leaned into him.

And his fate was sealed.

He heard a slight moan escape her lips as she drove her fingers into his hair. The sound of pleasure mingled with surrender inflamed him. He could feel his pulse accelerating and his heart hammer a wild tattoo.

Looking back later, he had no clear recollection of how they got from the threshold of her living room to her bedroom. He was only vaguely aware of an odd two-step of sorts, his mouth still sealed to hers, moving ever forward in slow motion as she stepped back at the same pace. Along the route, pieces of clothing rained down. His shirt, her blouse, his belt, her skirt.

When Kasey stepped out of her shoes, the jolt separated them for a second. She was close to four inches shorter in her bare feet.

Why that made his heart race even more, he hadn't a clue. Feelings of protectiveness sprang up out of nowhere, emerging out of the shadows. He found himself wanting to take care of her, to shield her from whatever it was that created that guarded, wary look in her eyes.

* * *

This is a mistake, a mistake, Krys, you know it is. Damn it, stop now!

And yet, she couldn't, which made no sense to her. She would never have let herself go like this with someone she hardly knew, and yet, she couldn't stop herself, couldn't pull back.

Didn't *want* to.

She needed and *wanted* this. Needed to feel like a woman again if only for a few precious minutes. That hired killer had robbed her not only of Jim and her life, but of everything else, as well, including her feelings. She hadn't allowed herself to feel *anything* all these long months. She desperately wanted something, at least one thing, back, if only for a handful of minutes.

She wanted to feel again.

Concerns were shed as swiftly as her clothing.

Her body heated, urges and desires taking over common sense.

If pressed, Kasey couldn't have said exactly what there was about this man that fired up her attraction. All she knew was that, deep in her soul, it had been almost instantaneous, even though she'd tried to ignore it, tried not to pay attention when she felt something inside of her igniting.

The life she led now was such that primal and basic instincts had shut down. Or so she'd told herself, but obviously, she'd lied. Because whatever was going on inside of her now was beyond her ability to regulate, to bank down and vanquish.

And it was very, very primal.

Startled, Kasey sucked in her breath as his lips and tongue expertly claimed her, branding her everywhere they touched. It seemed that incredible sensations were born in the wake of every caress, every pass of his hand, his mouth.

She felt delicious sensations slamming into her, making her peak over and over again. And still it went on. Firing her blood, making her feel almost dizzy and definitely giddy. Zack kissed the side of her neck, the inside of her elbow, the soft, vulnerable area between her breasts. She was like a mindless piece of cotton, eagerly absorbing everything that came her way.

Kasey arched her body, bringing it up closer to him. Wound her arms around his neck, pulling him down to her. All the while wanting more from his touch.

Even in her heated haze, Kasey knew this was never going to happen again, not with him, perhaps not with anyone. Certainly not for a very long time. She desperately needed to store up the memory of the explosions, of the sensations, to have them last her for as long as was humanly possible.

His body was hard against hers, demanding and yet, he seemed to be taking his time even as an urgency continued to fill her. With each passing moment, she found herself aching for that final, fulfilling release. But Zack continued to stroke, to caress, to fondle, kissing her and basically turning her into a mass of shimmering, uncontained longing.

She tried to return the favor as best she could, give

a little of the fierce pleasure that Zack created within her. She had no idea that the strength of her reaction to him was accomplishing just that for Zack.

There was supposed to be nothing new anymore, but this he recognized as being new. At least for him. She made him want to continue doing this forever. He gloried in bringing her from one shuddering climax to another. Her pleasure was his, twofold.

He'd never been aware of himself or the woman he was with, no matter what her attributes had been, as much as he was right at this very moment. Oh, there'd been women who'd been more beautiful, more agile, more schooled, but none had ever been more sensual, or moved him the way that this one did.

She was nothing short of magic, he thought, reveling in the feel of her flesh against his palms, the taste of her skin against his lips. She arched against him, offering what he wanted so badly to take.

He very nearly did just then.

But patience was something he had learned to incorporate into everything he did a long time ago. Patience made the outcome that much sweeter, that much more rewarding. It had been an edict he'd lived by all his adult life.

Patience, he discovered tonight, was also very hard to hold on to when its converse, *im*patience thundered through his veins, demanding the ultimate release, the ultimate joining of two bodies. Of two souls.

Unable to hold himself in check a heartbeat longer, Zack shifted his weight, covering her body with his. He touched his mouth to hers and then drove himself into her. Even that required restraint because he didn't want to take the journey alone, didn't want to leave her stranded by the wayside as he took his pleasure. It wasn't about him. Or even just about her. Perhaps for the first time in his life, it was about them.

Sheathed within her, Zack moved his hips with a growing urgency that she reflected back at him like a mirror, matching him thrust for thrust until it felt as if they really were one complete being. Kasey wrapped her legs around him.

The road grew steeper, the ascent sharper, the climb more intense until finally, he felt the final explosion, felt her tightening around him, tasted the whimper of pleasure as it escaped from her lips only to be smothered against his.

He tightened his arms around her even as the sensation began to settle into his bones, spreading out.

It was only a matter of time before it began to grow fainter.

With all his might, Zack wanted to hang on to the feeling, on to her, for as long as he possibly could. There was something overwhelmingly warm about the feel of her heart pounding against his chest. Mimicking the rhythm of his own heart.

Two hearts beating as one. The notion was so damn corny…and yet, also so very comforting. How was that possible?

Zack took a deep breath, raised himself up on his elbows and then slowly rolled off her. But rather than get up, the way he knew he should, the way he always had before, all he wanted to do was lie beside her. To hold her to him and pretend that all was right with the world instead of the exact opposite.

She wanted to hang on to this, to him, to the sparks that still danced and throbbed throughout her body. Such an incredible feeling of well-being, of content-ment, coursed through her veins. Feelings she had been so certain were lost to her. Except that here they were, alive and well. And back.

It was enough to make her want to cry.

But even as she struggled to tighten her grip around these elusive feelings, she could detect the glorious euphoria. Soon she would only have the memory of the deed itself.

She'd made love with a stranger. Sold herself out for the price of an ethereal high. Worse, she'd sold out Jim's memory. Betrayed him. The guilt all but choked her, creating an incredible lump in her throat. She could hardly draw breath. What she did was draw away from the man next to her. Shrank back, actually.

Oh God, what had she allowed herself to go and do in the name of need?

Wasn't she made of sterner stuff than that? Since when was she driven by a need for sex? Because that was what it was, sex, pure and simple.

Well, maybe not so pure and not really all that simple, but it was sex nonetheless.

When he tried to slip his arm beneath her, she pulled

back. He could almost read the regret in her eyes. But that would spoil it, he thought. And he didn't want it spoiled.

He tried again, this time a little more forcefully, and slipped his arm beneath her, pulling her gently to him. He raised his head and pressed a kiss to her forehead. "No regrets," he told her.

The action had been so tender, she could feel tears springing up in her eyes. Damn it, she hadn't cried in all these months, why now? Why in front of him, this stranger who seemed to know all the right buttons to press to completely unravel her?

"I feel like I'm coming apart," she told him, her voice thick.

"You were very, very together," he assured her. "And you can only come apart if you let yourself."

She tugged the edge of the comforter over herself. It didn't help. She might be covered, but she still felt utterly naked. "What makes you think you know me?"

"That's the part I can't explain. But I do. I might not know your background, or where you came from, or who your last lover was, but I know you. There's something inside of you that speaks to me."

"This line work for you?" she asked flippantly. "To help you pick up women?"

"I have no idea, I've never said it before. And you're not the type to say lines to," he added.

"I had a fiancé," she said suddenly, sitting up and bringing her knees to her.

He found himself looking at her naked back. Found

himself having the same urges that had stormed through his body earlier, as if they'd never been attended to.

She used the word *had*. Relief scurried through him. "What happened?"

"He was killed. Right in front of me."

He thought of his own life. Of the world he knew. "Was he a cop?"

"No." She'd already said too much. It wasn't safe to tell him. For both their sakes. "I don't want to talk about it anymore," she said suddenly, turning to him. Letting the comforter pool at her waist. "Make me forget, Zack. Make me forget I ever saw anything."

Pulling her down to him, he switched places until he was looming over her. "I'll do my best, Kasey," he promised just before he brought his mouth down to hers again.

Chapter 8

The tinny, melodic sound scissored through her dreamless sleep, drawing her to the surface.

The moment her eyes opened, Kasey bolted upright.

That was a phone ringing. Hers? No one had her number except for Edwin and he was still out of the state. She doubted if he'd be calling her at this hour.

But who else would be calling her? Unless...

What if they'd tracked her down?

Adrenaline raced through her veins as half-formed thoughts and fears vied for space in her head.

Then her surroundings sank in.

She was in her bedroom. And she wasn't alone.

Fear ratcheted up to another, more extreme level. And then she remembered last night. All of it. And Zack.

It was his phone, not hers, that rang.

Kasey released the breath she was holding.

Awake at the first ring, Zack tumbled out of his side of the bed, searching for the source. The last time he'd seen his phone, it had been in the front pocket of his jeans. The jeans he had kicked off somewhere between here and the back door.

After locating them, he dug into first one pocket, then the other before finding his cell phone. He flipped it open and placed it against his ear. Snapping out an irritated "Yeah?" he listened in silence to whoever was on the other end of the call.

Slowly he returned to the bed and sat down on the edge. His back was to her, but she was well acquainted with tension when she saw it. This wasn't a casual call.

A girlfriend?

A wife looking for her husband?

He could be someone's other half. What was it she knew about him anyway, other than the fact that he had made the world stand still for a little while?

Kasey drew the comforter around her just as she heard him sigh and say, "Right. I'll be there." He punctuated the promise by snapping his cell phone closed again.

Jeans still in one hand, the phone in the other, Zack turned around. He had to go. Even so, the same kind of longing he'd felt last night stirred the moment he looked at her. Making love with Kasey hadn't tempered that desire one iota. If anything, having her only heightened his need for more.

With effort, he banked it down.

Or tried to.

"I've got to go," he told her.

"Emergency?" she heard herself asking stiffly.

So much for not prying, she thought ruefully. She'd made up her mind that last night had been an aberration, "just one of those things." That meant she had no right to ask him questions and he had no right to ask her anything.

And yet the first thing out of her mouth was a personal query. What was wrong with her?

"Friend in need," he corrected, lying. He wouldn't have called the captain a friend, unless he employed the broadest definition of the word, and he wasn't heading out to come to Valdez's aid. He was heading out—if he ever got his pants on—to do his job. The net around the elusive computer identity thieves was about to be closed and he needed to be there to insure that the thieves didn't suddenly pull up stakes and disappear the way they already had twice before in the last twenty-one months.

This was his setup and he needed to be there for the takedown.

Almost as much as he *wanted* to be here.

Kasey glanced at her watch. It wasn't even four in the morning. What kind of people did he know? "I guess that qualifies you as friend of the year."

Did she believe him? Or did she think he was lying to her? And why did it even matter? But it did. He didn't want her to think of him as a liar, even though, technically, he was. But not by choice.

Zack tried to sound as sincere as possible. "I owe them a favor."

"But you don't owe me an explanation," she inter-jected, absolving him of the need to say anything further, truthful or otherwise. "I didn't mean to make it sound as if you did," she apologized with a hapless shrug. "I'm afraid I haven't had much practice at this two-ships-in-the-night kind of thing."

She was giving him a way out, he thought. A way to end this liaison without having it get messy. Except that, it occurred to him, he didn't want it to end, at least not yet. He wanted to see her again, be with her again. More now than before. That was unusual in itself. Or-dinarily, once he slept with a woman, all sorts of concerns began to slip in, which made any relationship difficult. He had his demons to wrestle with, demons he feared would emerge once he became comfortable with a woman. So he didn't let that happen. Instead, he would begin winding things down, taking down tents, doing everything it took to move along.

And yet here she was, pointing him toward the road, making it easy for him—and he didn't want to go.

Zack zipped up his jeans, then leaned over the bed. He slipped his fingers through her hair, cupping her head and tilting it up toward him. He smiled into her eyes.

"My ship would like permission to return to the harbor sometime very soon." He'd almost said "tonight" but something had stopped him. Instinct, he supposed. Not the self-preservation kind but one that told him he'd be moving too fast for her if he came back tonight. Even if he could manage that.

Fear and delight played tug-of-war within her. She

squelched both. In all likelihood, Zack was probably just saying that, she thought. It was a line, like "I'll call you," and meant nothing except to clear away any awkwardness for the time being.

Still, a grain of hope beat within her breast as she said, "All right."

She didn't really believe him. He could see it in her eyes. And suddenly, he *wanted* her to believe him. He needed to say or do something to convince her that he wasn't just talking. And then it came to him.

"How do you feel about weddings?" he asked as he picked up his shirt from the floor and put it on.

Kasey's mouth dropped open. "Excuse me?"

Maybe he should have started out with an explanation, he upbraided himself. But he was pressed for time, so he talked fast.

"My mother's getting married next week. It's going to be a big family thing. The groom's got enough family to populate a medium-size village." And most of them were in law enforcement, but he kept that to himself for the time being. "Anyway, I thought maybe," his fingers flew along, closing buttons, tucking in his shirt, "if you weren't busy, I could bring you with me."

"To your mother's wedding," Kasey said, trying to decide whether or not she believed him.

Was this all just a ruse to allay any suspicions she might have? Or was he coming on strong? She honestly didn't know which side she was rooting for, if any. While she missed taking part in any actual day-to-day

life, suddenly being pulled back into it made her feel
somewhat uneasy. Unprepared. She'd gotten rusty.

And if it *was* on the level, she felt a twinge of guilt over
immersing herself in his family while allowing her grandmother to go on possibly believing that she was dead. Oh
damn, what she wouldn't give for life not to be this complicated, to be filled with grueling, spirit-draining thirty-
hour shifts at the hospital and nothing else.

Studying her reaction, Zack debated withdrawing
the invitation. He didn't want Kasey to feel pressured.
But just as quickly, he decided against rescinding the
invitation. He *wanted* her to come and meet his people.

Maybe he was growing up—or just going through a
phase, he amended, mocking himself. Either way, he
wanted Kasey there with him.

"Yeah, to my mother's wedding. I think you'll enjoy
yourself—or, at the very least, see that you didn't have
such a deprived childhood after all. My brother and
sisters will be there."

She didn't give him an answer right away. Instead,
still wrapped in the comforter, she eased off her bed and
accompanied him to the front door.

"So what do you say?" he asked, turning toward her
at the door.

"Go help your friend, he's waiting for you." Kasey
realized that she'd made an assumption about the caller.
Maybe it hadn't been a man, but a woman who needed
him. "Or she's waiting for you," she said.

"He," Zack told her, reading between the lines.
"It's a he."

She nodded and tried not to grin. "Okay, he's waiting for you."

His eyes held hers. He wasn't leaving until he had an answer. "That's not what I was asking about."

Her expression was just a touch rueful. "You mean the invitation."

He put his hands on her bare shoulders. The temptation to draw away the comforter was hard to resist, but he held himself in check because if he followed through, he wasn't going to make the bust, not for a good long while.

"Right."

The opportunity to be normal, to share a normal event with normal people was too much for her to turn down. Kasey could literally feel herself weakening until she gave in. The entire process lasted approximately thirty seconds.

"You're sure your mother won't mind?"

He was the son Lila McIntyre—soon to be Cavanaugh—despaired of. He never brought anyone around for her to meet. This, he knew, would be a welcomed reversal of behavior.

"My mother will be thrilled," he promised her.

Kasey's mouth curved. "All right, then, I'll go with you to thrill your mother."

His margin of time was evaporating. He should have already been behind the wheel of his car and on his way to the scene of what Randall, the mastermind of the tristate gang, thought was going to be the site of his greatest triumph. Even if he left this second, he was going to have to bend all the speed limits from here to his destination.

But he didn't want to leave without kissing her one more time.

He allowed himself no more than thirty seconds. Any longer and he wasn't going anywhere.

"Great." The single word described both his satisfaction with her answer and his reaction to kissing her goodbye. Because it wasn't a parting kiss. To him, it was an invitation for more. A great deal more.

As he hurried out her door, Zack found himself really looking forward to that.

Kasey didn't go back to sleep after double-locking the door in Zack's wake. She'd actually tried, for about fifteen, twenty minutes, but she knew the effort was doomed to failure. She was too keyed up to drift back to sleep for even a few minutes. The man had left her far too stirred up even *before* he'd kissed her goodbye.

Was this a mistake, getting involved with Zack? she wondered as she took one of her quick, three-minute showers. And just who was she getting involved with anyway? Someone who got mysterious phone calls in the middle of the night, phone calls that had him running off into the darkness without much of an explanation.

For all she knew, he could be a drug dealer. After all, he had gotten shot the first night she'd found him. And he'd never volunteered what he did for a living.

Because you didn't ask.

Even if she had, would he have told her the truth? she wondered. Or would he have come up with some sort of plausible lie? Did he lie for a living? Was he a fugitive, a criminal?

You're a fugitive, remember?

Drying off, she stopped to hold her head as questions multiplied inside, taunting her. Oh God, she was tired of being distrusting. Tired of being cut off from life in general. Well, she wasn't all that cut off from life last night.

She went to her closet and pulled out a simple black pencil skirt and a black-and-white pullover. Moving to the bureau, she took out fresh underwear and began getting dressed.

Kasey paused for a moment, remembering. Reflecting. She had no idea what to make of or call last night, other than pure ecstasy while it was happening. He'd made her body sing, made her soul get lost in sensations, some of which she'd honestly never experienced before, despite the fact that she had always thought of Jim as a consummate lover.

Would there be consequences for last night? Was she letting her guard down too fast?

Maybe he hadn't crossed her path by accident, maybe it had all been orchestrated to seem casual, but wasn't.

Maybe—

She yanked her pullover over her head, angrily punching her arms through the capped sleeves. She felt like a ball at a tennis match, battered from one side to the other and then back again.

Enough.

"Damn it, Krys, you've read too many mysteries, seen too many movies. Things aren't usually as complicated as all that," she told her reflection as she pulled a brush through her hair. She was making up scenarios in order to push Zack away.

Because she was scared.

Scared to feel and risk losing again.

Was it better not to have anything to lose? The end result was the same: emptiness.

"Get over yourself," she told the reflection in the mirror. She put the brush down and peered closely at her image, checking her roots. Looking for a telltale sign that would give away her true color. But they were still dark. She was still all right. For now.

After giving herself a last once-over, she went to the kitchen for some coffee. She still had a bookstore to open.

There were times when being a patriarch had its drawbacks. Looking back, Andrew Cavanaugh could hardly remember when he wasn't the one in charge, whether of the entire police force, or of his own mushrooming family. Most of the time, that suited him just fine. He liked it that way.

But every so often, he became acutely aware of the burden, not just the joy.

As he looked at his nephew Patrick, his niece Patience and their spouses, it occurred to him that most of the discomfort he faced as head of the family had to do with his younger brother Mike.

This time was no different, even though Mike was

dead and had been for years. He was still cleaning up Mike's messes, still trying to smooth out incredibly challenging situations.

He didn't want to upheave these young people's lives, but he had no choice. *Mike* had left him no choice.

As far back as he could remember, even when he was a boy, Mike had made it known that he felt short-changed by life. He never seemed to understand that anything worth having had to be earned. Mike never saw what he had accomplished, only what he hadn't.

For the most part, Andrew knew that his younger brother felt overshadowed both by him and by Brian. Hell, it was easier to complain about circumstances than to try to rectify them. Or make his own unique imprint in the world.

Mike preferred complaining and losing his soul to a bottle.

Looking back, Andrew had to admit that Mike had been a malcontent. His jealousy made him not the easiest man to get along with. Though he didn't want to admit it at the time, Andrew knew that Mike had even tried to break up his marriage by trying to get his wife Rose to run away with him. Whether his brother wanted to do it because he was really in love with Rose or for revenge, Andrew didn't know.

But despite all these flaws and shortcomings, never in his wildest dreams would he have suspected that Mike would have fathered a second family. Not only that, but Mike had cut the children and their mother off entirely, leaving them all to fend and provide for themselves. And ultimately leaving it up to him to find a way to bring about a reconciliation, Andrew thought now. Because that was what he was bound to do. To bring them all together.

In this whole world, nothing was more sacred to Andrew than family. Even family on the fringe, the way these three young individuals who had sought him out currently were. They deserved better than the kind of treatment they had received at Mike's hands. And he meant to see that they got it.

Damn it, Mike, what were you thinking?

Andrew had begun the process of assimilation slowly, by first telling Brian. Now it was time for the next step. Letting Patrick and Patience know that they had siblings they'd never known about—and at the same time finding a way to make that acceptable to them.

Nobody ever said life got easier.

Patrick looked over at his sister. They'd been sitting here for several minutes and neither of them had a clue why their presence had been requested like this out of the blue.

"So what's the big mystery, Uncle Andrew?" Patrick finally asked. "Why did you ask to see Patience and me and no one else?"

Andrew took a deep breath, then chose his words carefully. Patience and Patrick were going to be hurt, and possibly angry—at least Patrick was. But he wanted that anger channeled in the right direction and not against the three who had come to him.

"Because I thought you two would want a chance to get used to the idea before we told the others."

"What idea?" Patience asked. "You're really being very mysterious about this, Uncle Andrew."

There was no way to say this but to say it, he decided. His gray eyes swept over the young man and woman who he loved like his own. The two to whose aid he'd come more than once when Mike was in a particularly ugly mood.

"I wanted you two to meet someone. Actually, three someones." Aware that Patience and Patrick eyed him, more confused than ever, he raised his voice a little, calling into the kitchen. "Ethan, Kyle, Greer, could you come out here please?"

"Who are Ethan, Kyle and Greer?" Patrick asked. The next moment, his attention was drawn to the three people who entered the room, shepherded in by his aunt Rose. About to say hello to his aunt, the word faded from Patrick's lips. His wife's hand tightened on his, but he was barely aware of it. Barely aware of his sister's sharp intake of breath, as well.

He felt as if he was looking into a mirror that had somehow gotten stuck several years in the past. The two men looked like he had when he was just out of college. The young woman was a younger version of Patience.

"Patience, Patrick, I want you to meet Ethan, Kyle and Greer. Your half brothers and sister."

Chapter 9

The silence in the room was deafening and seemed endless. Mike Cavanaugh's old family stared, dumbfounded, at his new one—and vice versa.

And then Patrick broke the silence as he turned toward his uncle. "How long have you known?" he asked, his voice low, as if trying to contain his temper.

Andrew met his nephew's heated demand. He didn't blame Patrick for his reaction. This was a hell of a piece of news to take in.

"A couple of weeks."

Feelings of being betrayed materialized out of the shadows. "And you didn't tell us?" This time Patrick didn't bother hiding the accusation in his voice.

Andrew was the one person they'd counted on for the

truth. Andrew was the father he'd always wished he had. Now he wasn't so sure.

"I was looking for the right way to break the news to you and Patience. Obviously I didn't find it."

Shock might have been restricted to one side of the room, but anger wasn't. It was obvious to Andrew that the newcomers felt it, too.

Kyle squared his shoulders as he turned to his brother and sister. "Let's go."

"Hold it," Andrew ordered, moving into the center, between what had swiftly become opposing sides. There was no mistaking the authority in his voice. While he shot a silencing look toward Patrick, his words were addressed to the trio he'd asked to his house for this meeting. "Declaring your existence is not a bad idea. Getting the family together as a whole is not a bad idea—"

Kyle cut the former chief of police short. "Then why's he looking at us as if we've just crawled out of the gutter?" he demanded, waving a hand at Patrick.

Andrew could see both sides. Sympathize with both sides. It was up to him to reconcile those sides and make them whole. "Maybe because Patrick had thought he'd seen the worst that his father could do, and to his devastation has just discovered that there was more."

Greer moved forward. Of the triplets, she was the most even-tempered, but this situation tested her. The last one born, youngest by five minutes, she was still exceedingly protective of her brothers.

"Are you saying that fathering us was the worst thing

that Mike Cavanaugh ever did?" Even now, a month after being told who their father really was, the man's name felt awkward on her tongue.

"No." Patience spoke before Andrew could answer. "But keeping you a secret all these years was." Rising from her seat, she came forward, her hand extended to this young woman through whose veins her father's blood ran. "Hi, I'm Patience."

Greer looked at her half sister's hand for a long moment, trying to come to grips with such a wealth of emotions zigzagging through her that she couldn't begin to sort them out. Finally, drawing in a long breath, Greer took the offered hand and wrapped her long, slender fingers around it.

"Greer," she said.

It occurred to Greer that she no longer knew her last name. For twenty-three years, it had been O'Brien, her mother's name. But with her mother's deathbed revelation about their father, did that make her a Cavanaugh now? Or was she still an O'Brien?

"I'm Greer," she repeated, trying to muster a smile.

"And I'm sorry, but I'm out of here," Patrick said abruptly as he turned on his heel and headed toward the front door.

"Patrick!" Maggie cried. But he gave no indication that he heard her. "He doesn't mean it," Maggie told the three people next to Andrew. "This is just a little hard for him to take in."

"Welcome to the club," she heard one of the two men mutter. On her feet, Maggie quickly went after her husband. She managed to catch up to Patrick just as he was about to go out the front door. "Patrick, wait."

"Don't apologize for me, Maggie," he snapped without turning around.

Maggie shoved the door closed, cutting him off from his avenue of escape. "Well, someone has to when you act like an idiot." A former internal affairs officer, she knew what it was like to be on the outside through no fault of her own, what it felt like to be distrusted. "You think this is easy for them? Facing you? Carrying that stigma of being your father's bastards?" she demanded.

When he turned from her, she deliberately shifted so that she was in his face. She loved Patrick far too much to allow him to appear to be cruel. She knew him better than that. The man withdrew in order to protect the boy.

"Give them a chance, Patrick. Be fair." Her voice softened. "Be the man I fell in love with." She gave him an alternative. "If you want to be angry, be angry at your father."

The anger in his eyes would have had her backing away if it wasn't so important to stand her ground. "You think I'm not?"

"Actually," she replied with a sigh, "I think it's rather pointless to be angry at him, even though I suggested it." After all, the man was dead. There would be no restitution, no remorse, or even any explanations forthcoming from that quarter. "From everything I've heard about Mike Cavanaugh since joining this family, your father carried around a lot of demons that he never could come to terms with." In a way, she rather felt sorry for the man. He was tortured his whole existence. But her main objective was not to allow Patrick to be dragged down by his father's actions or his influence. "He was one unhappy man."

Patrick laughed shortly. "Didn't exactly make life a picnic for the rest of us, either."

A broad, encouraging grin curved the corners of Maggie's mouth. "And yet, you and Patience turned out just fine."

"That was mainly because of Uncle Andrew." Andrew, who interceded every opportunity he got, who separated his sister and him from both his parents those times when his father became a particularly ugly drunk.

"Uncle Andrew," she repeated. "You mean the man you just walked out on?"

Patrick frowned. Leave it to Maggie to be the voice of reason. To make him ashamed of losing his temper without saying a single accusing word. Damn, what would he do without this annoying, wonderful woman?

He looked down at her. "You think you've won this argument, don't you?"

Maggie threaded her arm through his, smiling up at his face. "Yup. Now let's get back in there so nobody suspects how damn pigheaded you can actually get at times."

Patrick laughed softly. "I think Patience already knows."

"Yes," Maggie agreed, "but Patience is a good soul. She'll take that little secret to her grave. Now try to smile," she encouraged. "You look really fierce when you frown."

"Never made an impression on you," Patrick pointed out.

"That's because I'm fearless," she told him brightly just before they walked back into the living room.

"Change your mind?" Andrew asked mildly, glancing at his nephew.

"Changed his heart," Maggie corrected.

Andrew nodded. "It was always a good heart. Now then," he said, turning toward the others, "let's get acquainted over some lunch."

This time, there were no dissenters.

"So how do you feel?" Andrew asked, popping his head into the tiny room to check on his brother the following Saturday afternoon.

In his estimation, Brian had never looked better. Not even at his first wedding. Despite their trials and tribulations, the years had been good to Brian, making him look more distinguished and downplaying the wild, mischievous boy he'd once known him to be. Downplaying that facet, but not altogether doing away with it. All Brian needed to do was smile broadly and the boy he'd been was right there, in his eyes.

Brian took in a deep breath. It didn't seem to help. His nerves were a tangled web of wet spaghetti. He looked at Andrew's reflection in the mirror. "Like I'd rather face down a boatload of Columbian cocaine smugglers armed with AK-47s."

Andrew stepped into the small room just off the altar. Several feet beyond that, the church, bedecked with pink-and-white carnations, smothered in sprigs of baby's breath, filled up with family and friends who had come to bear witness to this happy occasion.

But within the tiny room, the tension was palpable.

Noting that Brian's bow tie was slightly askew, Andrew carefully adjusted it, shifting it a micro-inch to the side. "I'm sure that little comment would warm Lila's heart if she'd heard you."

Brian stared up at the ceiling as his brother fussed over him. "Has nothing to do with Lila."

Andrew's eyes met his. "She's the one you're marrying."

"Yeah, about that." Brian cleared his throat nervously. He'd never thought about being old, but maybe he should have. Marriage was for the young, not the young at heart. "Do you think I'm being a fool?"

"No more now than usual." Andrew stepped back, and then grew serious. "But if you let Lila go a second time, then yes, I think you're being a fool. Brian, this is the woman you were meant to be with all along. No disrespect to your late wife, but Lila's so much more of a true fit for you than Susan ever was. Lila's your soul mate. Just like Rose is mine." Putting his hands on his brother's shoulders, he turned and pointed Brian toward the door. "Now get out there," he urged. "Before Lila comes to her senses and makes a run for it."

"Right," Brian said with renewed feeling, his cold feet becoming a thing of the past. But he paused for a second, looking at his brother. "Thanks for being there, Andrew."

Andrew grinned, slapping him on his back. "It's

what I do. Just remember what you just said the next time you get mad at me. Now let's get out there and get you married."

He gave Brian a little push out the door.

Zack glanced toward the bride's side of the church and was relieved to see Kasey still sitting where he'd placed her. Their eyes met and he smiled. He would have wanted to enjoy the ceremony sitting beside her, but Brian had asked him to be part of the wedding party, which meant that for the duration of the ceremony, he and Kasey would be apart.

And he would be unable to stop her if she suddenly changed her mind about being here and left.

So far so good.

Standing at the altar, listening to Father Scanlon say the words to eternally tie his mother to Brian Cavanaugh, Zack silently admitted that his attention was diverted. He only half heard the priest as he kept his eyes on Kasey. And thought again how fantastic she looked.

The ankle-length teal-blue dress adhered to her every curve. Kasey had literally taken his breath away when she'd first opened the door to admit him to her house earlier today.

Two hours later, he still hadn't caught it back yet.

Try as he might, he couldn't remember feeling this way about a woman before. He'd made a point to avoid feeling this way about a woman, afraid of where it might lead, what it might bring out in him.

Though he tried to ignore its existence, there was this nagging sensation buried deep in his mind that was steadily moving forward, demanding attention. Reminding him that he was his father's son and as such, he needed to be on his guard to keep from losing his temper, to keep the consequences of that loss in check. Because apples, he'd heard time and again, didn't fall far from the tree.

Which meant that he was an abuser waiting to happen.

He couldn't imagine anything worse than acting like his father toward someone he cared about.

"Hey," Frank whispered, nudging him. "We're supposed to follow Mom and Brian." He nodded toward the procession that now departed from the altar. "Where *are* you today?" he hissed.

"Thinking about the case," Zack muttered, falling into place beside Brian's daughter, Janelle. It was a lie. The case was over, but it was the best he could come up with on the spot.

"Not with that goofy look on your face," Frank contradicted. They stopped just outside the carved double doors as guests armed with cameras snapped memories from all possible angles. "Not that I blame you." Frank looked over his shoulder into the church as the last of the pews were being emptied. The woman he'd seen earlier with Zack made her way forward. "Nice-looking lady. Don't remember you ever bringing one around before." He looked at his older brother, quite impressed. "Is she on the job?"

Frank asked him if she was part of the police force.

He hadn't even told her that he was with the Aurora police department. "No. She works in a bookstore."

Frank grinned. "She looks like the intellectual type," he teased. "She teaching you to read?"

Zack gave him a look. This was Frank's not-too-subtle way of prying. "What she's teaching me is none of your business."

Frank laughed, reading between the lines. "Oh, it's like that, is it?"

Zack was about to answer when he heard Janelle laugh. He'd been paired up with her as they'd marched down the aisle. He eyed her quizzically now.

"Sorry." The apology was for eavesdropping. "It's just that you sound like one of us already. If I closed my eyes, I wouldn't be able to tell you two apart from my brothers." Still beaming, obviously delighted to see her father this happy, Janelle rose up on her toes and kissed Zack's cheek, then shifted over toward Frank and repeated the gesture. "Welcome to the family, boys. Like it or not, you're Cavanaughs now—no matter what the name on your badge says."

He was about to say something in response when a movement out of the corner of his eye caught his attention. Or maybe it was the vivid color of her dress that pulled his attention toward Kasey. She'd been coming toward him, but then abruptly stopped. She looked utterly stunned.

Had she overheard Janelle's comment about his badge? It didn't matter any longer if she knew since as of yesterday afternoon, he was no longer operating undercover. The identity-theft ring had been effectively smashed and about half a million people would be receiving notices from the police department that they were the victims of an elaborate scam.

Now he was free to admit he was a detective attached to APD's fraud unit.

Was it his imagination, or had Kasey suddenly gone pale? He watched as she headed toward a side exit.

"Kasey. Kasey, wait up." He glanced over his shoulder at his brother. "Tell the others I'll catch up to everyone at the reception."

"What about pictures?" Janelle asked.

"I'll make it in time," he promised.

Right now, he needed to stop Kasey. Working his way through the last of the wedding guests, Zack hurried after her. He had nearly a foot on her and his legs were a lot longer. It didn't take much for him to catch up to her, despite the fact that Kasey had quickened her pace.

"Kasey, damn it, wait," he called again. Why wasn't she listening? He caught her by the arm and pulled her around to face him. "Where are you going?"

She didn't know where she was going. She didn't have an escape car. Zack had been the one to drive them here. All she knew was that she needed to get away, go somewhere quiet so that she could think. Damn it, she'd been blindsided. And now, it was useless to try to pull free. Instead, she went on the attack. It was all she had. "You're a cop?"

She'd snapped out the words as if they framed an accusation. It made him acutely aware that there was so much he didn't know about the woman he found so attractive.

He continued to hold on to her arm, afraid that she might bolt if he let her go.

"Yeah, I'm a cop." His eyes searched her face, trying to make sense of her reaction. "I take it you don't like cops."

Kasey's eyes narrowed. Why hadn't she trusted her instincts? They'd warned her he was too good to be true. "You lied to me."

"No," he corrected patiently. "I didn't lie, I just never told you what I did for a living. But I would have lied if you'd asked me," he admitted honestly. "I would have had to," he explained. "I was undercover. But I'm not anymore."

When he'd showed up at her door, shaven and in a tuxedo, she had literally felt her heart skip not one but several beats. But she'd attributed his clean-shaven appearance to the fact that he was in the wedding party, not that some secret operation he'd been assigned to was over.

Her reaction to his work had been almost violent. Why? Had she been arrested? Done time? Had someone she cared about been harassed by the police? Or had she been harassed? There was more than one bad apple on the force, no matter how much they cleaned house. Had she had a run-in with one of them that had tainted her forever?

"You have something against cops?" he asked again, his tone as far from confrontational as humanly possible.

A sinking feeling twisted her stomach into a tight knot.

Yes, a cop killed Jim. Would have killed me. I don't trust them. I don't know if I can even trust you.

But she couldn't say any of that, because even telling him that would have meant trusting him and although a part of her desperately wanted to, she wasn't ready to take that step just yet.

Maybe she would never be.

"No. I just have something against being held in the dark. Lied to by virtue of the sin of omission," she elaborated heatedly.

"I couldn't tell you who I was then without jeopardizing the case I was on. I wasn't the only one involved." He might be willing to risk his own life, but there was no way he would risk the lives of the men who'd gone undercover with him.

She could use this as an excuse to flee. To be alone again. But the words wouldn't come. God help her, she didn't want to be alone again. "And that's over with now? The undercover thing?"

He nodded. In the distance, he heard a car honking. Were they calling him? "Yes."

"Is that why you were shot?" she asked.

"Yes."

"Who shot you?"

"Doesn't matter now." He slipped his arm through hers and began to lead her toward the front of the church. There was now an unobstructed path. Everyone had gone outside. "What matters is that I don't want the fact that I'm a cop to drive you away." He knew women who would have nothing to do with someone on the force because the risk of being a widow was so high. Was that what was stopping her? "I think you should know, though, that this is a family of cops. On both sides," he added. "In that church, you were one of the few civilians in attendance."

That would explain the uneasy feeling she had the minute she'd walked in, Kasey thought. Though all that had gone down had happened in another town, still one of the people here might know who she was. The odds were against her.

The knot in her stomach was back.

Chapter 10

Try as she might to fade into the woodwork at the reception, Kasey found that she couldn't.

For one thing, she wasn't dressed for the part of a shrinking violet or a wallflower. The slinky gown she wore turned heads in her direction no matter where she went. For another, the people at the reception were far too friendly and outgoing to allow her to stand quietly off to the side—even if Zack had abandoned her, which he hadn't.

For one length of time he was forced to leave her side because the photographer had insisted on taking formal photographs of the wedding party. But even then, Zack made certain that she wasn't alone. Before joining the others, he entrusted her to the care of one of Andrew Cavanaugh's daughters, a very savvy, bright-eyed woman named Callie.

Like her siblings and most of her cousins, Callie was a detective, too.

After the proper introductions, she couldn't help wondering who was keeping the streets of Aurora safe. Over half the police department was present here at the community center that Andrew Cavanaugh had reserved for his younger brother's wedding.

She began to think Andrew was one amazing man. He'd organized the entire reception within a very short space of time. The air at the community center was filled with voices, good cheer and the delicious aroma of the meal that Andrew had stayed up half the night preparing.

Everyone, absolutely *everyone* was friendly toward her. She'd expected it from perhaps Zack's mother, and possibly his new stepfather because she assumed the man wanted to make points with his new stepson. But even after Zack returned to her side and they sat down at one of the many tables, an entire legion of people seemed to stop at their table to say a few words to Zack and to her.

And it wasn't even the inane chatter of strangers, restricted to "Hello" "How are you?" "Isn't this a nice wedding?" or stilted words to that effect. The conversations, short or long, were genuinely warm, teasing and personal.

It all underscored Kasey's feelings that she had really missed out by not being part of a large family.

Early in the festivities, Zack's sisters, Taylor and Riley,

both eye-catching blondes, swiftly appraised her without actually appearing to do so. Each sister in turn told her that she felt honor bound to share at least a few of Zack's bad habits. There seemed to be enough so-called flaws to go around because neither sister repeated herself.

His brother, Frank, was different. He didn't come by baring "secrets" about Zack. He stopped at their table to put out feelers. A charmer, it was obvious that Frank was a lover of women. Many women. She had no doubt that they loved him right back. Quick to laugh, he was more outgoing than Zack, more lively. And, she suspected, possibly less solid.

You sound like you're intending to build a lifetime with the man, instead of just getting through the evening in one piece, the voice in her head taunted.

Before she could silence it, Andrew Cavanaugh crossed the floor and presented himself at their table. The man was everywhere at once, overseeing the food, seeing to the wedding guests' comfort and still finding time for small talk as he wove his way in and out between the tables.

Reaching theirs, he clasped Zack's hand in both of his and shook it heartily as if he hadn't just seen him at the church and then for the duration of the wedding photos.

"Welcome to the family, boy. A lot of new additions this month," he commented, nodding at the table where two young men and a young woman, all incredibly similar-looking, were seated. Then he glanced in her direction and nodded his head, as if she were included in his sweeping statement. Warm approval flared in the man's crinkling smile. "I've gotten seven new nieces and nephews without even trying," he chuckled.

It amazed Zack how accepting the man was. He'd heard through Dax, Brian's son, about Patrick's father's indiscretion and the trio who had resulted from it. Despite the uncomfortable situation, everyone in the Cavanaugh family was taking to the newcomers—not to mention to him and his family.

There was a lot to live up to, becoming a Cavanaugh, he thought. But rather than feeling as if the task was daunting, he couldn't help but welcome the challenge. They were damn good people.

The head of the "good people" looked at him intently at the moment. "Where are your manners, son?" Andrew prodded. He inclined his head toward Kasey. "Aren't you going to introduce me?"

Andrew knew exactly who the woman sitting beside him was. Just because he didn't drive to the police station every day didn't mean that he had lost his edge, his connection. Andrew made a point of knowing everything.

But for the sake of being polite, Zack indulged the man and made the formal introduction. "Andrew Cavanaugh, this is Kasey Madigan. Kasey, this is—" He paused for a moment, as if weighing the word he was going to use. "My new uncle Andrew."

Andrew laughed, clapping him on the back. "Good answer, boy."

"Uncle Andrew's responsible for this reception," Zack told her. Dax had told him about the huge breakfasts Andrew always made, summoning as many of the clan as could come. He'd been told that now that he was one of them, his appearance was expected at least several times a month. He'd also been told that the trip was well worth it. "He likes to cook."

"I prefer to say I create," Andrew told Kasey, enveloping her hand between both of his as he gently shook it.

She gazed at the older man in surprise. "Then you're not in law enforcement?" she guessed.

Andrew had left the force to care for his five children when a freak accident had everyone but him presuming that his wife was dead. He took early retirement to raise his brood and to look for Rose. He succeeded in both endeavors.

"Not anymore," he told Kasey.

"But he used to be the chief of police in Aurora," Zack added. And, rumor had it, a great deal more capable than his successor.

"Oh." So he was one of them, too. Was it her imagination, or was the older man peering at her as if he was trying to place her?

The next moment, her suspicions were confirmed. His eyes on hers, Andrew asked, "Do I know you?" He released her hand, still studying her face. "You look very familiar."

If Frank had said that, she would have taken it as an opening line. But she knew Andrew meant the phrase as it sounded. That her face had nudged something in the recesses of his mind. Had he seen her picture somewhere in connection to the slaying she'd witnessed?

With effort, she shrugged off his question. "I have that kind of face. People mistake me for someone else all the time."

"The face of an angel," Andrew commented.

"I've only been in town for a few months," Kasey continued, ignoring the compliment. She was completely focused on making Andrew believe that he was wrong about knowing her from somewhere. She didn't want him trying to remember where he'd seen her.

Andrew sensed the tension in her voice, even though he assumed she probably thought she had it under control. He'd questioned too many suspects in his career not to be aware of it. That kind of an instinct followed you to the grave.

But for now, there was no reason to make her uncomfortable. It would come to him. It always did. "I'd better make sure the next course is ready on time," he said, taking his leave. He nodded at Kasey as he backed away. "Nice to have met you, Kasey."

"Likewise," she murmured, forcing a smile to her lips. Ordinarily, she would have meant that. Andrew Cavanaugh seemed very likeable. But something in the older man's gray eyes told her he wasn't about to give up trying to remember where he knew her.

Was it time to move on again?

She realized that Zack was talking to her. Rousing herself out of her fear-laced mental fog, she looked at him. "I'm sorry, I was just thinking."

The way she had been all evening, Zack thought. But

there was no point in saying something like that. She'd only deny it. Pursuing the matter would only lead to an argument that he definitely didn't want to have. She might appear sensual and sexy, but underneath all that, the woman was hiding something. He'd bet his life on it. He didn't want to scare her away before he found out what.

"Would you like to dance?" he asked, inclining his head toward the small orchestra that played.

There was a time when she loved to dance. Love to give herself up to the music and let it move her. Now, it was all about control, about keeping her guard up, not drifting off in a man's arms.

What did she expect to happen here? Someone from the D.A.'s office to appear and serve her with a subpoena? She was getting carried away again, she silently upbraided herself. She had to see the upside of things. Being in a room full of police personnel meant that no one was going to take a potshot at her, no one was going to attempt to blow her away in case she was tempted to once more risk becoming the D.A.'s star— and now only—witness in the murder trial.

She knew that without her they had nothing. The killer would walk. Jim's killer would walk. But if she came forward again, she might not ever make it to the trial and the case would disappear again. The mob's reach extended everywhere. If she wanted to live, she had to keep on hiding.

But right this minute, she was safe. For now.

"I would love to dance," she told him, pushing back her chair and rising.

Zack had been prepared to coerce her. Her answer surprised him. Smiling, he took her hand in his and made his way to the dance floor.

He was aware that they were garnering looks as they walked by. Or rather, she was. Not that he could blame anyone. In a room full of attractive people— and the Cavanaughs all seemed to be damn good-looking, he'd noted—Kasey Madigan still managed to stand out.

And she danced like a dream, he thought several minutes later.

Or maybe he was the one having the dream, Zack amended as he held her hand to his chest. His other hand was pressed against the small of her back, just where the dress dipped low. He held her to him, so close that her body all but melded into his—the way it had the night they'd made love.

He wanted to make love with her again. To celebrate his case going down successfully. To celebrate his mother marrying a good man.

To celebrate having Kasey in his life, he thought, smiling warmly into her face.

"What are you thinking?" she couldn't help asking.

That I want to make love to you all night. "About how life surprises you sometimes," he said, doing his best to quiet his racing pulse. "You think you know every-thing, have everything pretty much mapped out for yourself and then, just like that, it all changes on you. And brings you a surprise all tied up with a big red bow." He realized that there were tears shimmering in her eyes. Oh God, he hadn't meant to make her cry. "Did I say something wrong?"

"No," she answered a little too quickly. "Something nice."

His words were wonderful. It wasn't his fault that they described both the best event in her life—and the worst. Because she'd made plans with Jim, happily-ever-after plans and just like that, they were changed. Snuffed out. And just when life was at its bleakest, draining her of all hope, of ever even feeling anything again, Zack had stepped into it. Just like that, there were possibilities.

A glimmer of optimism wove a bright, silver-threaded tapestry of hope inside of her. Maybe she'd finally be safe here. Maybe she could finally stop running, stop always looking over her shoulder, anticipating the worst.

Apparently Zack's entire family, not just the new branch but his own immediate small group, including his mother, was in law enforcement. If she couldn't find a measure of safety here amid this fortress of police personnel, then she would never feel safe anywhere.

It was something to cling to. At least for the time being.

Kasey went on dancing with Zack, allowing herself to relax. Allowing herself to dream.

She knew he would be coming home with her. Knew he would be staying.

At the start of the wedding, when he'd picked her up,

she'd tried to come up with a nice, plausible way to beg off. It was the sensible thing to do, to discourage him. But now, when the moment of truth had arrived and Zack was standing behind her, watching her unlock her door, she didn't want to send him away.

She didn't want to be alone. She'd been alone much too long.

Maybe she was living in a fool's paradise, or maybe this laxness had something to do with the three glasses of champagne she'd consumed. Kasey didn't know. Moreover, she really didn't care.

She just wanted to have Zack beside her one more night. Wake up with him next to her one more morning.

And pretend that this was something that would continue for her indefinitely.

After unlocking the door, she removed the key, slipped it back into her purse. She closed her purse and then looked at him.

No words were necessary. The invitation was there in her eyes.

Zack followed her inside and the second the door was closed again, he framed her face with his hands, brought her mouth a little closer to his and then eliminated the small distance between them altogether.

He kissed her with all the longing that had built up these last few hours, that had escalated to dangerous proportions while he'd been dancing with her.

When he'd held her in his arms on the dance floor, they'd each been inside the other's shadow. So much so that his body had pulsed wildly with growing desires and demands.

The way it was doing now.

Except that now, he didn't have to try to hold it in check.

The shimmering teal dress peeled away from her like a wrapper, slipping to the floor as softly as the sigh that escaped her lips. Beneath the clinging gown she wore thigh-high stockings, sheer black underwear smaller than a whisper and nothing else.

His eyes swept over her with deep appreciation. She could have brought a dead man back to life. And he was far from dead. The pounding in his chest attested to that.

"God, but you look like every man's fantasy-come-true."

Her eyes on his, Kasey pulled out the decorative pins that held up her hair. Freed, it fell in cascading dark waves about her shoulders.

Mesmerized, Zack felt his breath growing short. He couldn't remember ever wanting a woman as much as he did right this moment.

"As long as I'm yours," she murmured.

The wide, appreciative grin that curved his lips almost overwhelmed her. Like the force of an arrow released from a crossbow, it went straight to the heart she'd thought she'd buried eighteen months ago.

"My thoughts exactly," he told her.

But when he went to enfold her in his arms, Kasey stopped him. He thought she'd changed her mind at the last minute, but then, to his relief, she swiftly went to work separating him from the tuxedo he still had on.

With a laugh, Zack started to help her and their fingers got in each other's way. So Zack retreated, raising his hands up in the universal gesture of surrender.

"You do it," he told her. "You do a better job of it anyway, and besides," he added, nuzzling her, "I like feeling your hands on me."

Why that bit of information should ramp up her excitement, she couldn't have said, but there was no denying it. So much she could hardly contain the eagerness thundering through her veins.

She did her best not to tear away the fabric, but the desires she experienced made it difficult.

Zack stepped out of the last of his garments, then took Kasey by the hand, leading her slowly into the bedroom.

And suddenly, there were no barriers, no scraps of clothing to get in the way, no excuses to stop what was inevitable.

They came together like two lovers familiar with each other's bodies but still eager for the thrill as they touched, caressed and reexplored terrain already claimed as all brand-new.

To her joy, Zack made love to every part of her.

And as he did so, he found he wanted more. Wanted to hear her cry out his name again after he'd brought her up to a climax using only his tongue and his lips. Wanted to feel her arch her flesh against his suckling mouth again. Wanted to feel the desire shoot through him as she spread a network of small, openmouthed kisses along his belly and lower torso, branding him the way he had branded her.

They left nothing untouched. And finally, when they both felt as if they were on the edge of exhaustion, they came together and discovered another wealth of energy for the last conquest. For the last trip to the highest summit.

When the climax came, Kasey prayed it would never let go. Prayed that this wondrous space of time would somehow be eternal. She was willing to die since she was convinced it couldn't possibly get any better than this.

Chapter 11

Jeremy waited until Zack was directly in front of him. "You know I can get into trouble for this. We both can," he said in a low voice.

The lab tech had summoned him with a three-word message: *I've got something.* Zack had broken a speed record getting down to the forensic lab. Jeremy's statement wasn't news. Zack already knew the man was climbing out on a limb. He gave Jeremy a safety net.

"The woman was part of the case I was working on." Granted, it was a stretch, but there was a germ of truth in his statement. "I had to make sure she wasn't part of the people we were after," he added to bolster his claim. Jeremy began to look just a shade less nervous. "She did turn up rather conveniently less than half a mile away from where Seales shot me."

Jeremy was silent for a long moment. "That's your story, huh?"

Zack nodded without cracking a smile. "Yup."

Jeremy blew out a breath. "Okay, works for me. Anyway, she doesn't look as if she's part of anything. Matter of fact, the DMV doesn't even have Kasey Madigan's thumbprint."

But that didn't make sense. He'd seen her driving, although she always had him drive when they were together.

"She said she traveled around. Maybe she still has her out-of-state license," Zack speculated. But even as he said it, he wasn't convinced. She'd said something about being at the bookstore for over five months. Wouldn't a person exchange her license after five months?

Unless she wasn't planning on staying, Zack realized.

"Maybe," Jeremy allowed loftily. It occurred to Zack that Jeremy seemed pleased with himself. "And maybe she shares a thumbprint with a dead woman."

Zack stared at the tech. "Come again?"

Excited, Jeremy picked up speed as he went on with his explanation. "When I didn't find 'Kasey Madigan's' prints on file anywhere, not even the DMV, I remembered this show I saw on one of those cable channels. You know," he couldn't help inserting the small sidebar, "the one that treats forensic lab technicians as if they were gods instead of flunkies—"

Zack knew what was expected of him. He gave

Jeremy what the man wanted to hear. A little ego stroking. "You're not a flunky, Jeremy. You're an important member of the team."

Getting his due, Jeremy continued. "Anyway, I ran her thumbprint through the DMV's deceased database and guess what? Your lady's been dead for almost two years now. Not only that, but when she was alive, she had a different name."

For a split second, there was a strange ringing in Zack's ears. Moreover, an eerie feeling came over him. As if everything had just stopped dead for him. His heart, the air, time, everything had just shut down. This couldn't be right.

Oh no? Then why are you here? Why'd you ask Jeremy to see if he could lift any viable prints off the book? Why'd you even take the book in the first place if you had no doubts?

He banked down the annoying voice in his head. "What name?" he asked.

With a flourish, Jeremy turned his LCD monitor toward him so that he could see the license for himself. "Krystle Maller. She was a doctor, too." Jeremy turned the monitor back around again.

Damn it, she'd lied to him. Lied. The word throbbed in his head. "How did she 'die'?"

Jeremy shook his head. "I don't know yet, but I can probably—"

Zack raised his hand to stop the flow of words, and any further action. "That's okay, Jeremy. You did good. I'll take it from here."

Jeremy looked a little let down as well as confused. "You're sure?"

"Yeah," Zack said. "I'm sure." Whatever he found out, he didn't want it out in the open where he couldn't control it. Not until he knew what to make of it all.

Now that he had a name, tracking down more information wouldn't be that difficult. He wasn't one of those people who could make a computer tap dance and sing or coax the Internet to surrender all its secrets, but he knew someone who could.

Ironically, because of his mother's marriage, they were family now, which gave him an in. He knew exactly who to approach for help. Or actually, it would be her husband he'd go to first. While the Cavanaugh family numbered several computer experts in their ever-increasing numbers, none was as incredibly proficient at getting technology to do her bidding as Dax's wife, Brenda.

Murmuring "Thanks, I owe you one," to Jeremy, Zack walked out, completely preoccupied. He had a problem. The problem didn't involve approaching Brenda. He knew where to find Dax and everyone within the family was more than generous. His basic problem was deciding just how much he wanted anyone else to know about the situation.

He was going to have to level with Dax and Brenda. But he honestly didn't know how he felt about all this. It had hit him too fast, too hard. One minute, he was up so high, there were clouds passing beneath his feet and now he was so low, he was buried six feet under without the benefit of a funeral service.

The woman had turned him inside out.

Granted, he admitted again as he walked down the corridor and to the elevator, if he hadn't been the slightest bit suspicious that something was off, he wouldn't have taken the book with her prints in the first place. That was his police training coming to the foreground. His gut instincts demanded that all bases were covered.

But those instincts were nowhere in sight now. He had no idea what to make of the fact that "Kasey" had lied to him from the get-go. That everything she'd told him so far was most likely a lie, other than the fact that she worked at the bookstore.

Was the other night a lie, too? he couldn't help wondering. Had she made love to him with some ulterior motive in mind? Had she orchestrated all this to make him fall for her for some reason he was unaware of? Because he had. He'd fallen for her—and he felt like a fool. He was supposed to be smarter than this, more savvy than this.

Damn it, anyway.

"You're jumping to conclusions, Detective," he muttered solemnly as he entered the empty elevator and pressed one for the first floor.

He was convicting her without a trial. A glimmer of hope pushed its way forward—that would be his mother's influence. Maybe there was a logical explanation for all this. Maybe "Kasey" had been afraid to tell him the truth because, after all, he hadn't exactly made a sterling first impression, either. The first time she'd come in contact with him, he'd been shot, bleeding and unconscious, draped across the threshold of her back door. Not exactly his best foot forward.

But he'd made amends after that, he silently insisted. After he'd come around to the bookstore, and to see her, to take her out and to introduce her to his family. There sure as hell had been time for her to tell him the truth during all this and she hadn't. She'd kept up the lies.

Why?

And who the hell was Dr. Krystle Maller anyway?

"She was an eyewitness to a mob hit," Brenda told him later that evening as he and Dax stood behind her desk, watching her unearth the information.

Dax put a hand on her shoulder, a soft laugh escaping his lips. "We haven't called them 'the mob' for years now, Bren. They're referred to as 'wise guys' now."

Among her other talents, Brenda could speed read and she'd already skimmed the article. "Not very wise the way this thing went down," she commented, nodding at the article she had pulled up on the computer. "Seems like this Dr. Krystle Maller you're asking about was an unwitting witness, along with her fiancé, a Dr. James Strickland, to a 'wise guy' shooting. An execution, really. They went to the police and the D.A. had them both placed into protective custody until the trial."

Zack looked closer at the screen, scanning for pertinent details. "So what happened?"

"They're both dead," Brenda told him grimly. "James was shot in the hotel room where they were being kept. Krystle managed to escape, only to die in a house fire.

Apparently she must have come back to her house to get some things and someone torched it while she was still inside. The house was burned down to the ground before the fire department could reach it."

Zack looked at her. Maybe this was just a case of mistaken identity, a computer glitch, in which case, Kasey and this Krystle woman were *not* the same person. "They found the body?"

Brenda switched screens, going to the more recent article she'd pulled up. "They found *a* body but it was too badly burned for the coroner to make a proper iden-tification. According to the police report, one of her neighbors said she saw Krystle going into the house earlier. So the assumption is that her body was the one they found." Finished, she exchanged looks with her husband. Neither one of them liked evidence that couldn't be wrapped up tightly with a bow.

Dax turned his attention to his new stepbrother. "Why all the questions, Zack? You think you found this woman?" He tapped the screen.

Mindful of fingerprints, Brenda batted his hand away.

"I'm not sure," Zack hedged. He needed to see this thing through before he admitted the full story. He looked at Brenda. "Is there anything else?"

Brenda shook her head. "Not that I can see. But I can keep on looking," she volunteered.

"Does it say anything about her friends, her family?" Zack wanted to know.

She scrolled down on the first article. "It mentions a

grandmother. Delia Delaney," she read. "According to this, Krystle's parents were killed in a car accident when she was a little girl and this grandmother, Delia, raised her. Here," Brenda hit ctrl-P on the keyboard. Instantly, the printer came to life. "Let me print the articles up for you."

Zack nodded his appreciation. It didn't escape his attention that neither Dax nor Brenda put any real hard questions to him. He appreciated that. "You're the best, Brenda."

"I'm a Cavanaugh," she answered with a grin, glancing at Dax before retrieving the newly printed pages and handing them to Zack. She winked. "Being the best just goes with the territory."

Days afterward, Kasey couldn't seem to get the wedding reception out of her mind. Being at the festive family gathering had not only created a warm feeling within her, but had also woken up a tremendous yearning coupled with guilt. Her grandmother was at the center of both emotions. She missed the older woman terribly. Missed her and felt terrible about not having gotten in contact with her all this time, save for the one postcard.

Yes, it was for her grandmother's own protection, but she knew her grandmother would have chosen to be a little less safe if it meant seeing her, talking to her. Knowing firsthand that she was all right.

In that department, Kasey had the advantage over the older woman. If knowing someone was ill could be considered an advantage. Delia Delaney had to visit her nephrologist on a regular basis because her kidneys were becoming less and less efficient. Eventually, they would shut down. Because of her ability to unobtrusively hack into databases, something she'd picked up from a former boyfriend in college, Kasey was able to follow her grandmother's progress. It also alerted her to the fact that Delia's doctor had sent her to the hospital for observation a few days ago.

More than anything, Kasey wanted to go visit her. Wanted to hold her grandmother's hand and tell her that everything was going to be all right. But she also knew that her very appearance in her grandmother's room would complicate matters. For all she knew, the man who had ordered Jim killed had people watching her grandmother's every move, waiting to see if she'd "risen from the dead" and gotten in contact with the woman.

Even so, her heart warred with her head.

The fact that her grandmother was staying at the same hospital where she'd done both her internship and her residency, made it even more tempting to try to see her. Kasey even knew how to get in after hours via an entrance that the physicians used.

Kasey knotted her hands together, as if to seal in her emotions. No matter what *she* wanted, she couldn't take a chance on risking her grandmother's life. She had absolutely no doubt that if the man who'd had Jim killed knew she was alive, he would have her grandmother taken prisoner in order to flush her out. For the most part, the man obviously still thought that she was dead. So dead she had to stay.

Tears stung her eyes.

The small woman had two IVs, one in each arm, making them seem even more twiglike. Judging by the bump her torso made beneath the white blanket on her hospital bed, Zack estimated that she was no taller than five feet—if she stretched. Five feet and possibly ninety pounds or so. But her blue eyes sparkled when she smiled, reminding him of Kasey.

Holding up his ID and the shield that was pinned opposite it, Zack introduced himself for a second time. The first time, his name seemed to float right over the woman's head without being absorbed. She'd blinked, then asked him to repeat what he'd just said.

Delia Delaney nodded slowly at the name, then asked without embarrassment. "And do I know you, Detective?"

He tucked his shield back into the inside of his jacket. "No, ma'am."

The answer seemed to please her. At least she hadn't forgotten him. "A handsome young man like you should have better things to do than to hang around hospital rooms, talking to half-dead old women."

"Not at the moment," he answered truthfully. "And you're not half-dead, ma'am. Not with those eyes."

His comment widened her smile, just as he had hoped. Slipping his fingers into his pocket, he drew out the photograph that he'd had Brenda blow up. It was a picture of Kasey, taken at the wedding reception. Taken without her knowledge because every time someone had come around with a camera, she had deliberately turned away. Except once. And Dax had been the one to snap the shot.

Zack held out the photograph to her. "Mrs. Delaney, do you know this woman?"

Delia Delaney took the photograph into her paper-thin hand. He could have sworn he saw a flicker of something in her eyes for one unguarded moment. Happiness? And then, just as quickly, it was gone. Delia raised her clear blue eyes to his face. "Who did you say you were with?"

It had been on the shield. Was she stalling for time, trying to think? Maybe he'd been on the job too long. Maybe he was becoming too suspicious. Not everyone had a hidden agenda.

"I'm with the Aurora police department, ma'am."

The answer made the woman appear more confused. "But this is Kensington. Why would you be looking for my granddaughter in Aurora?"

"Then that's your granddaughter?" he asked, something inside of him sinking. He realized that until this moment, a very small part of him had been hoping for a miracle. Hoping that somehow, the computer had made a mistake and spewed out the wrong information for Brenda. Hoping that Kasey hadn't lied to him.

Bringing the photograph closer, she squinted. "No, I've made a mistake. That's not my granddaughter. That's not Krystle." She looked down at the photograph one last time before offering it back to him. "It couldn't be."

"And why's that?" he asked, taking the photograph from her. He held it in his hand rather than slip it back into the inside pocket of his jacket, keeping it in the woman's view. Maybe it would make her change her story.

"Because I'm afraid Krystle is dead. She died tragically in a fire that destroyed her house, as well," she told him softly, knotting gnarled fingers together on top of the bed sheet.

She sounded so sincere, so sad, he was tempted to believe her. If he hadn't seen that initial glimmer in her eye.

Delia took a deep breath, as if struggling to remain awake. "She's a pretty little thing, though. What's her name?"

The old woman was actually pumping him for information. He couldn't help being amused. "Kasey Madigan."

"Kasey," she repeated slowly as a smile that could only be described as nostalgic slipped over her lips. "My granddaughter used to love to play with trains—just like her father did as a boy, I'm told. I would tease her and call her my little Casey Jones. Casey Jones was—"

"I know who Casey Jones was, ma'am." A railroad engineer immortalized in a kids' song, as he recalled. He even remembered some of the lyrics.

"Good for you, Detective. Is this Kasey a friend of yours?" she asked, nodding at the photograph.

Something twisted in his chest. His heart? Or was that the thrust of the knife of betrayal? "I thought so. But apparently she's someone I don't know at all."

Delia took the information in stride. "This woman you think you don't know, is she well?"

"She is."

The woman nodded, pleased. "Good. Keep her that way," she entreated.

A tall order, especially since Kasey/Krystle didn't trust him enough to be honest with him. "I don't think it's up to me."

Delia reached out for his hand, placing hers on top of it for a moment. Her fingers were cold. "If you care for her, it is." She withdrew her hand again, letting it drop back in her lap. "It's up to all of us to look out for one another. People have forgotten that," she lamented softly. "I'm from a small town and we always watched out for one another. Can't beat that for a feeling of well-being."

He liked the old woman. He had a feeling that if his mother's mother had lived, she would have been just like Delia Delaney. Feisty and spirited no matter what life had decided to throw her way.

It occurred to him that he had tracked her down, but hadn't taken more personal things into account. "Why are you in here?" he asked suddenly.

Delia shrugged, her thin shoulders rising and falling helplessly beneath the hospital-issue gown.

"They tell me my kidneys don't want to obey me any longer. The doctor's doing what he can. My grand-daughter was a doctor, you know. A general surgeon." Pride radiated from every pore. "She was really something. You would have liked her," she told him with a knowing nod of her head.

The trouble was, Zack thought, he more than liked Kasey. And that fact had obviously blinded him to the truth.

"I have a feeling you might be right." He began to back away. "Well, I've taken up too much of your time already—"

"That's all right. I don't get many good-looking men visiting me, Detective…" Her voice trailed off expectantly.

"McIntyre," he supplied.

"McIntyre," she repeated with what he took to be an approving smile. "Take care of that friend of yours you were asking about."

"I'll do my best."

As he turned from the bed, he bumped into a nurse who was just entering the room. The photograph he'd been holding fell to the floor and the woman picked it up before he had a chance. She smiled at him as she returned it.

And then she turned her attention to Delia. "And how are we this afternoon, Mrs. Delaney?"

"*We* need to get out of this bed before *we* go crazy," he heard the woman answer.

Zack caught himself smiling. If Delia Delaney wasn't Kasey's grandmother, she certainly should have been.

Chapter 12

Zack found that it was hard keeping his feelings of exasperation, of betrayal, under wraps. For the first time, he had trouble focusing on his work. Now that the tristate identity-theft ring had been smashed, a ton of paperwork had to be addressed. It was the downside of police work that he vehemently disliked. Usually, he could get through it.

This time his mind insisted on going AWOL, returning to what he'd discovered with Brenda's help and what he'd wound up learning during his visit to Kasey's grandmother. That he had fallen—hook, line and sinker—for a fictitious woman.

The funny thing was, he still thought of her as Kasey, even though Kasey Madigan had never existed.

He'd been a chump right from the very start, he up-braided himself. His suspicions should have been aroused the moment he'd discovered that she had removed the bullet from his side and sewn him up with no problem. He didn't care how handy she was with a needle, that wasn't a skill you picked up from reading a book.

While it was hard for him to control his thoughts at work, it was even harder off the job. Harder still to keep everything in check when he was with her.

Zack had been with Kasey twice now since he'd dis-covered her true identity—and wasn't that ironic, he thought without a trace of humor. Here he was, just coming out of a clean takedown of a heretofore elusive gang that stole people's identities on a regular basis and the woman he was involved with had done the very same thing, taken on someone else's identity.

Except that it wasn't the same thing, he reminded himself as he lay next to Kasey in her bed, holding her to him. The thieves who were now in custody had stolen real people's identities to enrich their bank accounts and live off someone else's labor. Presumably, Krystle Maller had become Kasey Madigan just to stay alive.

Okay, giving her every benefit of the doubt—why hadn't she trusted him enough to tell him who she really was? Especially after he had told her that he was a police detective? That meant that he could protect her.

Hell, he *wanted* to protect her.

There in the dark beside her, it suddenly occurred to him that there actually was a good side to this. He'd come face-to-face with an entire spectrum of anger—

shock, betrayal, rage, even fury—and not once had he fought the urge to lash out at her physically, or even to become verbally abusive. Which meant that while he might be his father's son, that didn't automatically mean that he had inherited his father's violent tendencies.

The specter of fear he'd lived under for so long began to loosen its grip on him. If anything, his anger made him want to withdraw, to pull into himself and away from the source of his anger. The source of his pain.

But withdrawing was the same as running and *that* wasn't going to solve anything. And waiting for her to come to him on her own was, at this point, pretty futile. It was up to him to initiate the conversation that would, hopefully, cause her to finally come clean. Zack wanted her to have every opportunity to tell him on her own who she was. Though tempted, he absolutely refused to hurl accusations at her.

But waiting made him damn impatient.

Maybe she just needed to be encouraged, he told himself.

Tightening his arm around Kasey, Zack murmured against the top of her head, "You're awfully quiet tonight."

There was a very simple reason for that, she thought. He made her happy. Was she wrong, trying to catch a little bit of happiness for herself? Or was she being naive? Was this just the calm before the storm, the moment of peace before the other shoe dropped? She'd let her guard down before, trusted before, and wound up at the center of an unnavigable storm.

She desperately wanted to believe that history wouldn't repeat itself.

"That's because I've used up every ounce of strength, every last drop of oxygen, just trying to keep up with you."

She'd done more than try, he thought with a grin. Each time they came together was even better than the last.

Would this be the last?

If he started this, if he pursued the matter of her identity to its natural conclusion, would tonight be the last time they'd make love, lose themselves in each other's arms?

Fear of losing her reared its head and for a second, he thought of abandoning the course he'd just plotted for himself. Abandon it because he didn't want to lose being with her like this. It was far too precious—

But what did he have, really? A relationship with someone who didn't exist, someone who hadn't trusted him enough to give him her real name. Someone who could pick up and vanish the very next moment, moving on to be someone else.

He played the game a moment longer. "I'll go slower next time, so you won't lose your breath," he promised her.

"Don't you dare," Kasey laughed, turning her body to his. Her eyes swept over his face. "Don't you change anything about yourself."

Her words took him aback for a second. He wondered if she realized how ironic her statement was. He skimmed his thumb along her lips, wondering just what irony tasted like on her tongue.

It pushed him forward.

"You know, Janelle told me something interesting about a case a friend of hers had been on a while back." A slight puzzled look came into her eyes. He assumed the name meant nothing to her. "You remember Janelle, right? You met her at the reception. She's Brian Cavanaugh's only daughter and an assistant district attorney."

Kasey thought for a second, then nodded. "There were so many of them, it's still a little hard keeping everyone straight," she confessed.

Zack could have sworn he heard a wistful note in her voice. She wasn't faking that. She *did* want a family the way she'd told him. Maybe there hadn't been as many lies as he thought.

"Janelle said the case involved a doctor who had been the state's entire case against this wise guy kingpin, Carmine Pasquale. He killed the CEO of a stem-cell research firm late one night in a parking lot." He saw her eyes widen. Saw the light go out of them. He pushed on. "She and her fiancé were eyewitnesses to the hit. But the fiancé was killed soon afterward and, the story goes, the doctor died in the same fire that destroyed her house. The police determined that it was arson. No surprise there."

Kasey went completely cold inside. It felt as if an anvil had been dropped on her chest. She couldn't breathe. Sitting up, she drew the comforter close as she hugged her knees to her.

"Kasey?" Sitting up, Zack looked at her, concerned. He wanted to hold her, but for now, he refrained. Waiting.

There was no escaping her life, Kasey thought miserably. She'd been so sure, so very sure, that this time she'd succeeded in completely covering up her trail. That she was finally safe, finally free. And although the cost was a dear one—she could never see her grandmother again—at least she could gradually stop looking over her shoulder.

Obviously, she'd been wrong. Dead wrong.

"You know everything, don't you?" It was more a rhetorical statement giving voice to the terrible feeling that had taken her hostage.

The awful realization that she was going to have to go on the run again left her sick inside. If this man, who wasn't even trying, could figure out who she was, Carmine Pasquale could find her. She'd been fooling herself, thinking that faking her own death would take the heat off. Men like Pasquale took nothing for granted. He, or his representative, would be at her doorstep soon enough, caressing his weapon like a well-loved mistress trained to do his bidding.

It was only a matter of time before she was as dead as that CEO. As dead as Jim.

Unless she ran again.

She became aware that Zack still talked to her. His voice broke into her scrambled thoughts.

"Why didn't you come to me?" he asked.

He almost sounded hurt, she thought. Where did she begin? That initially she hadn't trusted him because she made it a rule not to trust anyone? And once she did trust him, it was too late, the lies she'd given him had been too convincing. Besides, why should she drag him into this? It wasn't his fight, it was hers.

"And say what?" she finally asked incredulously. "That I was really supposed to be dead, except that I wasn't?"

"No," he cut in impatiently. "Why didn't you come to me with the rest of it? That you were a witness to a murder? To two murders," he corrected himself, thinking of her fiancé.

Kasey shook her head adamantly. "No, Krystle Maller was a witness to a murder—an execution—and she died in a fire. That was supposed to be the end of it," she lamented.

"Except that we both know that she didn't die. Look, I can take you in, protect you—nothing's going to happen to you," he insisted. "Janelle can be the initial liaison—"

Protect her. She was not about to be taken in by those words again, not even if they were coming from Zack. Because she knew better.

"That's what they said to us the first time around. That we'd be protected and everything was going to turn out fine. Except that it didn't turn out to be fine. The police detective assigned to protect us was on Pasquale's payroll. He was instructed to take us out the first chance that he got. Jim died midsentence, asking him a question."

Zack watched as her eyes filled with tears. Reaching out, he tried to pull her to him, to comfort her as best he could. But Kasey pushed him back, keeping him at arm's length. She seemed determined to stand on her own as she recited the events.

Tears were falling and she brushed them away with the back of her hand.

"I couldn't even hold him one last time, couldn't tell him I loved him. Jim fell forward, blocking the detective's next shot with his own body while I ran out of the room. And I never looked back, I just kept on running." She looked at Zack pointedly. "I'm still running."

Her story moved him and he almost felt jealous of the dead man, that she had loved this "Jim" so much that tears still came to her eyes when she talked about his death. "It's time to stop," he told her firmly.

But Kasey shook her head. "Don't you understand?" she cried. Was the man made out of stone? Wasn't any of this penetrating? The moment they got wind of the fact that she was alive, there were people who would stop at nothing to kill her. *"I can't."*

"What happened to your house?" He looked at her intently, not wanting to believe what was going through his head right now. "Who really burned it down?"

Kasey didn't answer right away. Zack was smart, she thought. But then, she wouldn't have fallen for a dumb man. She loved his mind as much as she loved the way he made love with her.

"I did."

"And the body they found?" he pressed, his eyes never leaving hers. He refused to believe that she had deliberately killed someone to throw the killers off the scent. "Whose was it?"

She wasn't proud of this. It hadn't been her finest moment. But she wasn't going to lie to make herself come off better. "Some homeless Jane Doe slated to be buried in Potter's Field." If there had been at least one ounce of possibility that the woman could have been identified, she would have never taken the corpse. "I snuck the body out of the hospital morgue and put it in my bedroom." She closed her eyes, remembering. "Then I took a few mementoes and torched the place.

"I was pretty sure that the police would think that the so-called 'suspect' had someone set the fire to get rid of the only witness against him. I did it because I wanted to be free." She laughed shortly, shaking her head again. How could she have been so naive? "Instead, I'm more of a prisoner now than ever. The bars are just invisible."

She still hadn't answered the crucial question. "And why didn't you tell me?" he asked. "After we made love, why didn't you tell me who you really were?"

"It was a police detective who killed Jim. He was obviously on the killers' payroll."

She'd stunned him. For a second, he could only stare at her in complete disbelief. "And you thought that I was part of that?"

If she said yes, she knew it would really hurt him. But she couldn't deny it, either, because that would be lying. She glanced away for a second, addressing the air over his shoulder.

"The thing about being paranoid, there is no off switch you can hit."

Zack prided himself on his logic. If she felt one way, how could she then act in complete discord to her beliefs? It just didn't make sense. Had she been trying to use him? With every fiber of his being, he didn't want to believe that.

"But if you didn't trust me," he persisted, "why did you sleep with me?"

She spread her hands wide, as if the whole thing had been beyond her control. "Because you were—and are—just too irresistible," she answered simply. "And if I had made a mistake, if I was in fact 'sleeping with the enemy,' it was one hell of a way to go."

He didn't know if she was being flippant or straight with him. It really didn't matter. He loved her. Zack drew her into his arms. Somehow, he had to convince her that they were going to get through this. Convince her that she no longer had to run. "I'm not the enemy, Kasey—Krystle."

His effort touched her. She placed her finger to his lips to banish any further effort to use her real name. Her "other" name. She was his Kasey and she liked that. "You can call me Kasey. It's actually a nickname my grandmother gave me. It's from that old folk song about Casey Jones," she recalled fondly. Her grandmother had taught her all the words, then actually went out of her way to locate a CD of children's songs with that song on it. God, but she missed her grandmother. "I loved playing with model trains—like my father did— so she thought it was appropriate."

Listening to her relate the story, it was on the tip of his tongue to tell her that he'd gone to see her grandmother in the hospital. But something kept the words from forming. Instinct? He decided that he'd save that revelation for another time. Right now, there was too much coming at her at once. For the time being, he just wanted to make Kasey feel safe.

He had never wanted anything so much in his life. And there was only one way to accomplish that. By getting rid of the threat against her. That meant putting the men who were after her permanently behind bars.

He had a feeling they both knew that, but he said it out loud anyway. "You're going to have to testify, Kasey."

To his surprise, she balked. "No," she said adamantly. "Look, I want to do what's right, but I'm not ready to die yet." Especially not now, when she'd found someone who was important to her. Someone she could love—*did* love.

"The only way you can be sure that you won't be killed is by putting these men—and everyone who had a hand in your fiancé's murder as well as the execution of that CEO—behind bars." He looked at her intently. "You *know* that. While they remain free, they can hurt you—they can kill you," he emphasized even as his stomach twisted at the very thought. "And the more time goes by, the more of a possibility it becomes."

He heard her sigh and took that to mean she was weakening. Zack pressed his advantage.

"You're not alone in this anymore, Kasey. For one thing, you'll pretty much have the backing of a good portion of the Aurora police department. They'll be behind you—and in front of you," he added with an encouraging smile. "Between the Cavanaughs and the

McIntyres, you've got a substantial part of the force in your corner. And one thing I've learned even before my mother married Brian is that the Cavanaughs always stick together. The fact that we McIntyres do goes without saying."

"I'm not a Cavanaugh, or a McIntyre," she reminded him.

"But I am," he told her solemnly. "And I want to keep you safe." He took her hands in his. "I *will* keep you safe."

It was a sweet notion and she would have dearly loved to cling to it. But she had become a realist these last eighteen months, having made the jump rather abruptly that horrible evening.

"You can't become my personal bodyguard." He had a job, a life, she couldn't expect him to give up everything just so that she wouldn't be shot at.

"Who says?" he demanded. Before she could answer, he continued, "The captain owes me a slightly cushier assignment after the last bust."

He made her smile despite herself. "And you think guarding me is a cushier assignment?"

He pressed a kiss to her bare shoulder. "Well, right off the top of my head, I can think of a few nice perks that just might go along with this assignment."

She shifted so that her body was touching his. The warmth began to spread through her, not slowly, like heated molasses drifting through her veins, but quickly, like a wildfire searing through a dried section of the forest.

"Is this the way you conduct all your bodyguarding

details?" she asked, humor curving the corners of her mouth.

He pretended to think over her question. "Never actually had a bodyguarding assignment before." As he talked, he pressed small, stirring kisses along the hollow of her throat. "This would be my first, but yes, I think my way would have a lot to recommend it."

He was doing it again. Making her pulse race, making her want him. Erasing anything and everything that existed beyond her four walls.

"You know I can't think straight when you do that," she managed to get out, throwing back her head.

"Actually, I was counting on it." She felt his words rippling against her skin as he spoke. "There's no 'straight thinking' called for at the moment."

She was being snowed, Kasey thought. And she couldn't say that she didn't love it. "You are a wicked, wicked man, Detective Zack McIntyre."

Zack shifted his weight over, his body covering hers as he began to nibble at the delicate spot on her throat. Stars began to pop out in her brain, a whole host of beautiful, wondrous stars.

"Is that a complaint?" he queried in between anointing her flesh with the tip of his tongue.

She couldn't keep from squirming. Couldn't refrain from slipping back into that hot, delicious haze that he kept creating for her.

"Oh, hell no," she breathed even as her tongue seemed to grow too thick to wield properly. Knowing she was lost, she wove her arms around his neck, surrendering to the feeling. In her heart was the dark, growing awareness that this was probably the last time she would be able to surrender to him like this. "That was a compliment."

"Just as long as I know."

She thought she heard a low laugh accompany his words a heartbeat before the lightning made a reappearance, claiming her.

Chapter 13

Carmine Pasquale was a firm believer that patience was always rewarded. While others around him had gotten caught up in the fast-faster-fastest insanity that seemed to be the hallmark of the present generation, he was still old school and proud of it. You waited. And you watched. And eventually, things fell into place the way they were supposed to.

Deep down, he'd known that Krystle Maller wasn't dead. It had all been far too convenient when the "event" had occurred. The press and police had attributed the fire she was reported to have died in to arson and laid the blame on his doorstep, even though there wasn't a snowball's chance in hell that they could prove it. Not unless they planted the evidence and they didn't.

The thing was, he knew he hadn't done it and none of his people had stepped forward to take the credit. They were not a modest crew and they would have spoken up—if there was anything to speak of.

So, if the fire had been deliberately set and neither he nor any of his people were responsible, that only left one person who could have done it. The person everyone thought was dead. Krystle Maller.

It was the only theory that made sense.

In a way, Pasquale had admired her. It had taken guts to burn down something that meant so much to her. Nobody could accuse Maller of not having guts. He almost hated offing her.

But he had to. He had enough things to keep track of, enough balls to juggle and keep up in the air, without worrying about her someday deciding she'd had enough of hiding and coming forward.

So he'd set one of his boys up to keep tabs on the old lady. Maller's grandmother. It was the only long shot he had available to play. And in the end, his patience had paid off. He'd been right.

The old broad had gone to the hospital and his little runaway had sent someone in her place to see how Delaney was doing. The nurse he was paying off had been quick to report about the young detective and the photograph he'd brought of Maller. She'd seen it with her own eyes. She'd been well compensated for the information. And then she'd been taken care of.

He doubted if they'd find the nurse's body for a long time. He didn't like leaving any loose ends.

Which was why it was so important to silence Maller.

A little string pulling here, a little cash exchanging hands there, and he'd learned the identity of the man paying Delaney a visit. An Aurora cop by the name of Zack McIntyre. He'd put one of his best men on it and McIntyre had led Tony literally right to Maller's door.

Now all he had to do was make arrangements. Because he was personally going to take the woman out. Having an underling do the job wouldn't be showing the doctor the proper respect and despite popular belief there was honor to be found within his organization. Certainly within him.

Oh God, no, no.

The protest echoed in Kasey's head as she stared in total disbelief at the stick in her hand.

Please, dear God, it can't be true. It just can't. Heaven knew she had enough to handle right now, enough heartache to deal with without throwing this into the mix, as well. There just *had* to be a mistake.

She continued to look accusingly at the stick, willing it to turn another color.

Granted she'd been feeling sick these last few days, but she'd attributed it to the fact that, despite her stalling, she had to leave again. This time it would be Zack she'd be leaving behind instead of her grandmother. Zack who wouldn't know where she was going.

Even when she started throwing up, she thought it was due to her rebellious nerves. It wasn't like the other two times when she'd picked up to go. Those times, it hadn't mattered much if she stayed beyond the inconvenience of pulling up stakes, of having to once more go through all the contortions of creating a new identity. Truth of it was, she'd gotten pretty damn good at working software in order to come up with a fake driver's license. After all, in this day and age, proper ID was very necessary.

No, she hadn't minded vanishing those other two times. But those other two times, she wasn't leaving her heart behind.

The way she would be now.

But her early-morning communion sessions with the toilet bowl had nothing to do with the way she felt about leaving Zack. She was pregnant.

She had always dreamed about being pregnant. But not now, not now. How was she going to go on the run with a brand-new human being growing inside of her? And how had this happened, anyway? Despite the passion and the spontaneity of their lovemaking, she and Zack had taken precautions. Zack had been very considerate about that. It was one of the things that had endeared him to her. But nothing in the world was foolproof and obviously birth-control methods fell under that heading.

Tears filled her eyes. This was the wrong time, the wrong place in her life for this to be happening. How was she going to handle being a mother?

And yet, she knew she wasn't going to take the road that so many other women before her had opted to travel. For better or worse, this was her destiny. This was what was meant to be. She couldn't just wipe away this little person who had all but magically come into her life.

Somehow, she was just going to find a way to deal with this latest twist her life had taken, just as she had dealt with losing Jim and giving up her life, all because she'd been in the wrong place at the wrong time.

Maybe someday she'd be back here in Aurora. Back to show Zack his son or daughter.

But right now, if that baby had a prayer of coming to term and being born, she had to get out of here. The same instincts that had helped her flee from that hotel room the first time urged her on now. She couldn't explain why, but she just felt as if she *had* to leave.

Before she couldn't.

"I'm sorry, Zack," she murmured as she sat down at the small desk in her bedroom and began to write.

It was her farewell note. In it, she told him how much their time together had meant to her. How he had opened up the world for her. But that she had to go, as much for him as for herself. She asked him to think kindly of her every now and then, and told him to move on with his life, the way she had to move on with hers.

She did *not* tell him that he was going to be a father in eight months or less. That would all but guarantee that he would leave no stone unturned looking for her. She knew what he was like.

Funny how she'd become so knowledgeable about him in such a short amount of time.

"I'm really, really sorry," she said as a tear fell on the paper. She tried to dab it up as best she could. "But there's really no other way. You can't protect me. These people are much too powerful and if you could figure out who I was, then they can figure out *where* I am. I won't risk you—or anyone else in your family. If something happened to you or any of them, I would never be able to forgive myself. Please try to understand that this is for the best and please don't come looking for me. You'll never find me."

She was about to sign her name when she thought she heard a noise just outside the house. Everything inside of her froze. She was becoming progressively jumpier. Now that she was about to hit the road again, all her old quirks returned in droves. The fear, the uneasiness, the cold fingertips and the amplification of any noise she heard or thought she heard.

Maybe at the new place—wherever that was going to be—she'd get a dog. A big dog that would alert her to any strangers approaching. A dog that could protect her. Maybe that would make her feel more secure.

The way she didn't feel now.

There it was again, that noise. Was there someone walking by her window? Or was that just the wind through the trees and her imagination playing havoc with the sound?

Looking down at her arm, Kasey saw gooseflesh form. She took in a deep breath, trying her best to calm down. Maybe she should wait until morning to leave.

Morning, without night's shadows to fuel her imagination and make her feel as if every tree branch was the enemy. Everything always looked a lot better, a lot more hopeful, in the morning. Maybe she'd even pass by the store, tell Edwin she was leaving instead of just not showing up. She owed it to him. Edwin had been good to her.

There was a knock on her door.

Kasey's heart all but stopped beating in her chest. She remained where she was, in her bedroom, frozen in place as her mind raced to form options. Glancing at her bedroom window, she debated crawling out that way if whoever was at the door tried to break in—

She jumped when her cell phone rang.

Fumbling, she pulled it out of her pocket. And then exhaled a long sigh of relief when she saw the number on the LCD screen.

Zack.

She pressed the phone to her ear, trying to hear above the pounding of her heart. "Hello?"

"Why aren't you answering your door?" she heard him ask.

Her head jerked in the direction of the front door. "That's you?"

She heard him laugh shortly. "Who else were you expecting?"

Getting up, she crossed to her bed to get the suitcase she'd just finished packing. She shoved it into her closet and quickly pulled the wardrobe door closed again. "Nobody, that's just it. Aren't you supposed to be working tonight?"

"I am. But I'm not due in for another half hour. I thought I'd stop by to see how you were doing." She heard concern in his voice.

Guilt assaulted her, but she'd already made up her mind. Still, she didn't want to spring it on him just yet, not face-to-face. So she opened the desk drawer and swept the blue sheet into it, then shut it again.

"Fine," she croaked. "I'm doing fine."

"So does that mean you'll let me in anytime soon?" he asked.

"Oh, sorry. Sorry," she apologized again, striding across the living room to the front door. God, she was really rattled. Otherwise, she would have already opened the door for him.

Flipping the locks, she yanked the door, then fought the very real, strong urge to throw her arms around his neck. Part of her felt as if she'd already left and was even now yearning to see him again. The other part had never wanted her to leave in the first place. It was opting to stay and fight for this new life that she'd unexpectedly stumbled on. It made for a horrible internal tug-of-war.

Get a grip, Krys, she upbraided herself even as she forced a wide smile to her lips. A second later, her lips became otherwise occupied as Zack leaned in and kissed her. Tilted the scale a little further toward her staying in Aurora.

Taking a breath, her eyes momentarily shut to savor the sensation he always created within her, Kasey stepped back.

"This is a surprise," she said, opening her eyes to look at him. She'd deliberately picked tonight to leave because he'd told her he was working. She hadn't thought he was just going to swing by like this.

Zack lightly brushed his hand along her cheek. "Just making sure you're okay."

It was hard for her not to just blurt out everything when he watched her that way. Somehow, she held her ground, telling herself it was for the best. "Why wouldn't I be?"

Zack didn't answer right away. Instead, he stared at her for a long moment. His gaze seemed to penetrate her very brain. As if he had the ability to read her thoughts.

Now there was an unnerving notion. She had to stop letting her imagination run away with her, she silently chided. Zack was just a man.

But there was no "just" when it came to Zack. It was a case of bad timing. And now, there was no way she would allow him or any of his family to risk their lives for her. And Carmine Pasquale had a very long, long reach.

Zack didn't want her to think that he was undermining her ability to stand on her own two feet, to handle whatever she was confronted with. But that didn't change the fact that he was worried about her. For so many reasons.

"No reason," he replied lightly. "You just seemed very upset the other night." He slipped his arms around her, drawing her back to him. Fitting her nicely against his torso. "You realize that I should have been the one who was upset because you didn't trust me." Zack kissed her again, more languidly this time. "No more secrets, okay?"

The very air left her lungs as she forced out the single word. "Okay."

It killed her to agree, to lie again, when she was literally living a secret right now. Two secrets: the fact that she carried his child and that she was about to disappear again, both while smiling guilelessly up into his face and telling Zack only what he wanted to hear.

There's a very special rock in hell set aside for you, Krys. I hope you know that.

Releasing her, Zack looked at his watch. It was getting late and he needed to spell Frank. "I should have come earlier," he lamented. It would have given them more time together.

"Earlier I was working," she reminded him. "But why? What happened earlier?"

"If I'd come over earlier—and you were here," he added with a hint of amusement at her interjection as he let his finger trail along the tips of her hair, "maybe we would have had a chance to snag a little early evening delight."

Even as he said it, she could feel herself reacting to the thought of making love with him one last time.

Get over it. It's not happening. You need to go.

She smiled up into his face. "I would have liked that."

More than you could possibly know.

He stole one last, quick kiss and left her with a

promise. "Maybe I can come by later, after my shift is over."

Her heart quickened. He was coming back? How much time did that give her? She tried to sound calm as she asked, "When will that be?"

He thought about what he and Frank had arranged. "In eight hours."

Eight hours. She'd be long gone by then. The thought punched a hole in her stomach, filling the space up with incredible sadness. But she managed to keep a lid on it as she nodded.

"All right, I'll keep a candle burning in the window for you," she promised.

He laughed softly. "I think I can find my way without the candle."

There was something in his eyes, just for a fleeting moment. Something she couldn't begin to fathom. And an odd note in his voice.

Did he suspect?

No, that wasn't possible. There was no reason for him to think she was going to leave. She'd given him every indication that she intended to stay here.

"Good to know," she murmured. She suddenly rose up on her toes and kissed him one last, *last* time. The sadness within her widened to almost unmanageable proportions. Struggling not to cry, she threw her arms around his neck and deepened the kiss, putting her whole heart and soul into it.

Wanting him to remember this moment because it was going to be their last together.

No way would she be here when he returned from his shift. Even if she hadn't made up her mind already, he would have made it up for her. She didn't care if it was pitch-black outside, she had to leave almost as soon as he did. The longer she delayed her departure, the harder it would be to execute.

So she would just have to learn to live without him. She'd done it before she'd ever met him, no reason to think that she couldn't manage it again.

He drew back, as if sensing the tension that was coursing through her body. He cupped her face in his hand. "Baby, what's the matter?"

"Nothing." She tried to laugh off his obvious concern and make him believe that there was no reason for it. "I just realized I loved you."

The loaded word hit him like a ton of bricks. They'd never talked about this, not out loud. But she'd already placed it in the past.

"Loved?" he echoed, his eyes never leaving her face. "As in past tense?"

"Love," she corrected. "As in the present tense." Here, at least, she wasn't going to lie. She wanted him to know. To remember. To understand that she hadn't left because she didn't love him but because she did. "That doesn't scare you off?"

His smile was swift to take his lips. Swift and engaging. It was a huge responsibility to have someone love you. Six months ago, he would have been certain that the very notion would have made him take to the hills. But not now. Now, he embraced it. "Oddly enough, it doesn't."

She allowed a deep sigh to escape her lips. "It scares me," she admitted freely.

He didn't want her to be afraid. Of anything. Ever again. Zack caressed her face one last time. "When I come back, we'll see what we can do about that," he promised.

And then he was gone, retreating into the night. She stood there for a moment, framed in her doorway, until she heard his car start up. He was already too far away for her to see. With a feeling of overwhelming reluctance, she stepped back and closed the door. On him. On their life together. On her happiness.

He was gone. And in a few minutes, she would be, too.

Her feet felt like lead even though she knew she should hurry, just in case he'd come back. She couldn't go through that twice, silently bidding him goodbye even as she let him think that she would be waiting for him right here when he got off duty.

When he got off duty, she would be about four hundred miles away. She hadn't decided what direction yet.

Crossing back to the bedroom, Kasey had just opened the closet and taken out her suitcase when an uneasiness overtook her. She wasn't alone. Someone else was in the house.

She didn't know how she knew, but she did.

Kasey came to the only conclusion she could. "Zack?" she called out. "Is that you? Did you leave something behind?" Walking out of her bedroom, she came out into the living room.

And saw the man standing there.

It wasn't Zack.

Chapter 14

As her breath backed up in her throat, Kasey was instantly propelled back two whole years. Back to when she and Jim had turned the corner on that dark street, hurrying to the car they'd left parked several blocks from the theater.

They were just in time to see a tall, silver-haired, distinguished-looking man in the distance fire two shots point-blank into the man standing before him. The shooter had used a silencer, but the shots weren't silent enough. His face frozen in surprise, the victim sank to his knees even as his life swiftly ebbed away from him.

Stunned, Jim had shouted an indignant, "Hey!" toward the killer before she could silence him. Terrified, she'd grabbed Jim's arm and started running toward his car, dragging him with her.

They managed to reach it and get in before the silver-haired man—Carmine Pasquale, they'd later learned—hurried toward them. Jim was gunning the engine and peeling out of the lot before Pasquale could catch up. But not before the man had left a bullet in the rear windshield, narrowly missing the back of Jim's head. It had taken everything she had not to scream.

Six months later, Jim was dead, not by Pasquale's hand but certainly by his order. People on his payroll were everywhere. Thanks to him, she'd learned to trust no one.

And now Carmine Pasquale, dressed in a dark gray suit and striking blue shirt, was standing in her living room. She had no doubt the gun in his hand cost more than she paid for rent in the last six months. Rumor had it he believed in quality all the way.

Pasquale was smiling, but his eyes were flat. Seeing them had her blood all but freezing in her veins. He looked very pleased with himself. She didn't have long to wonder why.

"I knew you weren't dead. Something in my gut said you were a fighter. That you were still out there some-where, alive. And I was right." His eyes swept over her. She could almost feel them as he took appraisal. "You really are a smart little girl, aren't you? I almost hate what I'm going to have to do. But some things are inevitable."

Kasey could feel her adrenaline accelerating. Her eyes swept around the room, desperately searching for something she could use as a weapon.

Something. Anything.

"How did you find me?" Her throat felt so dry, she almost croaked out the question. Her voice broke in the middle.

The mirthless smile widened. His eyes seemed colder, if that was possible. "Nothing's too difficult if you have enough money. I had someone keeping tabs on your grandmother—"

Kasey stopped being afraid. Anger reddened her cheeks as his words penetrated. "My grandmother? If you laid a hand on her—"

His laugh infuriated her. "You'd what?" he taunted. "Scratch my eyes out? Honey, in case you haven't noticed, I'm the one with the gun, not you. You are in no position to threaten me."

And then Pasquale shrugged, as if giving in to some internal debate as to whether or not to put her mind at ease. He decided to be kind. There was nothing to lose by the gesture and he liked to think of himself as magnanimous. Besides, she wasn't going to be alive much longer. He could afford this.

"And for the record, nothing's happened to your grandmother. At least," he amended whimsically, "nothing I've personally had a hand in."

Kasey went very still. She wasn't even aware of breathing. Just what was he implying? "What do you mean by that? What's wrong with my grandmother?"

"Her kidneys are on the way out," he informed her, using the same tone he might have employed to tell her that the newspaper was late. "She's on a transplant list. Right now, she's still at the hospital." The smile on

Pasquale's lips turned malicious. "Didn't your boy-friend tell you?"

A strange buzzing echoed in her ears. This was becoming more and more surreal. What did Zack have to do with her grandmother?

"Tell me what?"

"That he's been to see your grandmother. He even took a picture of you to show her. To ask her about you. He's a lot more clever than he looks," Pasquale added, shaking his head as if the fact surprised him. "Delia told him you were dead. Sounded very convincing, too. But she's as sharp a cookie as you are. If I were a betting man," his mouth twisted in amused irony inasmuch as, under an alias, he owed the controlling portion of several casinos and was known to frequent the gaming tables on occasion, "I'd say she knows that you're alive." He laughed dryly at his own oversight. "I think maybe we should have asked your grand-mother a few questions eighteen months ago, right after the fire."

None of this made any sense to her. Why did this man know so much about Zack? She refused to believe that he was on Pasquale's payroll. There had to be some other kind of an explanation for his knowing all this, other than having gotten it directly from Zack. There just *had* to be.

"How would you know what my grandmother told him?" she demanded angrily.

The answer was so simple, it tickled Pasquale. It was always the simple things that everyone tended to overlook. For a moment he thought of not telling her, of letting her go to her grave, wondering. But he wasn't the kind of man who did things without taking credit for them.

"Let's just say I have some really nice sound equipment in your grandmother's hospital room. And there's this cute little nurse who has a weakness for pretty things that her salary just won't cover. Most people are very easy." Pasquale looked at her pointedly, losing some of the humor from his voice. "You should have been easy. You should have let me buy you off, Doc. Then you could have just gone on with your life."

She didn't believe him for a moment. "Then I would have already been dead," she contradicted.

He laughed again. "Like I said, sharp. You're right. But I wouldn't have been so inconvenienced." He took a step toward her, his gun raised. "Get on your knees, Doctor. If you don't fight this, I promise it won't hurt."

She had no idea where her courage was coming from. Maybe it had something to do with the baby she was carrying, the one who wouldn't get a chance to draw a breath if she died here tonight.

No, she wasn't about to make this easy for Pasquale. She wanted to live.

She raised her chin. "And if I don't choose to go gently into that good night?" Kasey asked defiantly.

He nodded his head. "Poetry. I like that. I like a well-rounded woman." Again, his eyes swept over her, as if seeing her for the first time. There was a note of regret in his voice as he said, "Too bad you and I couldn't have met under better circumstances. As to your question, if you don't do as I say, then you'll find out just how much pain the human body can endure before finally expiring." He cocked the trigger, pointing the weapon at her. "Now, what'll it be, Doc?"

Exhaling a long, shaky breath, Kasey began to lower herself to the floor. But instead of going down, at the last moment, she threw herself forward and grabbed at his knees, tackling him and bringing him down. The gun went off, emitting a little "ping" as a bullet went into the ceiling.

Pasquale shouted a curse as he went down, hard. He narrowly avoided splitting his head open on the edge of the coffee table.

Kasey made a dash for the door, but he grabbed her ankle and pulled her down. Crashing into a stack of books she'd brought home from the shop, she screamed, then grabbed the books and started throwing them as hard as she could at his head. One caught him just over his eye. He let her go and she scrambled away, losing a shoe.

Screaming an obscenity at her, Pasquale managed to get to his feet and lunge forward. This time, he grabbed a fistful of her hair and lost no time in yanking her down.

Reaching up, flailing, Kasey made contact with his face. The second she did, she raked her nails over it, then quickly stuck a thumb into his eye. Gasping in pain, he released her hair.

Kasey gulped in air as she made a dash toward the kitchen. She needed a weapon, something to make them equal. She frantically remembered the gun she'd hidden in the largest canister. She had to reach it.

The second she crossed the threshold, she heard two distinctly different shots behind her. Kasey stiffened, waiting for the impact. Waiting to feel the disabling heat of pain spreading over her. Waiting for the blood to appear on some part of her body.

But there was nothing.

Was she in shock? Had that anesthetized the pain? Or was she already dead and this was just a scene being played out on some higher plane as she made the transition from earth to another life?

The next moment, someone's arms closed in around her. There was a knife on the counter. She dove for it, but couldn't reach. The man behind her caught her wrist, trapping her.

"It's okay, it's okay."

She heard the deep male voice assuring her, but she couldn't recognize it. Couldn't absorb the words he was telling her, only the tone.

"He can't hurt you anymore, Kasey."

Zack!

A sob tore from her throat as she turned around and found herself looking up into Zack's face. Behind him, Frank checked Pasquale's prone body over for any signs of life. Frank raised his head and moved it from side to side.

"Someday, you're going to have to find the time to give me pointers and teach me how to shoot like that, big brother."

Rising, Frank came over to join his older brother, but his attention was focused entirely on her. "Are you all right? Kasey?"

She couldn't talk. Tears streamed down her cheeks as she finally nodded her head in response.

Slanting a look toward the body on the floor, a pool of red swiftly widening around Pasquale's upper torso, she forced the words out of her mouth. Words she'd dreamed about saying.

"Is he really dead?"

Frank smiled and nodded. "He's really dead," he told her gently.

She closed her eyes for a moment, struggling not to break down. Struggling not to cry. It was over. Finally over. She could have her life back. She could finally live again.

She felt Zack continuing to hold her as she heard Frank call in the incident. In a matter of minutes she knew her house would be filled with police personnel and members of the crime investigation unit. She didn't know if she was going to be up to that.

Right now, all she wanted was someplace to hide where she could come to grips with being on the brink of death, only to have, in the blink of an eye, everything handed back to her on a silver platter.

Well, not everything, she amended ruefully. Jim was still gone, there was no changing that. But everything else could be back in her life. Her grandmother. Her career. She could walk out her door without scanning the area in fear. Could walk outside without fearing that she was being watched. Followed.

Fresh tears gathered in her eyes.

She turned them on Zack. She owed him everything. And then it suddenly occurred to her that he
wasn't even supposed to be here. He'd told her he was
on duty tonight.

"What are you doing here?" she finally managed
to ask him.

Zack grinned, so thankful that he'd followed his
initial instincts. He didn't even want to think about what
might have happened to her if he hadn't.

"You know, that's been a recurring question in our
relationship. You keep asking me that. I've been
watching your place ever since I found out who you
were, and, more importantly, who was involved in this
case." When he'd gone to Janelle with a request, she'd
looked into the matter for him and said that the charges
against Carmine Pasquale had been dropped since there
were no witnesses against him anymore. That was when
he knew Kasey's life was in jeopardy. The matter
wouldn't change if she took off again. He was determined to keep her safe and in Aurora.

"And when he wasn't around, I was." Frank winked
at her and grinned. "Zack can be pretty persuasive when
he wants to be."

She looked from one man to the other. "But why?
Did you know something, hear something?"

"Just going along with a hunch," Zack confessed.
"Mostly, though, I was afraid you were going to take
off again." He curbed the desire to run his fingers along
her face, to reassure himself that she was actually safe.

"That you'd pull a disappearing act without telling me where you were going."

"So you spied on me?"

He couldn't tell by her tone if she was taking offense at that—he had two sisters, he knew women could take offense where none was intended—but all he could do was tell her the truth.

"Guilty as charged."

She released a shaky breath. She had a feeling there would be more where that came from until her insides finally stopped trembling. She offered a forgiving smile.

"Well, since you saved my life, I guess I can't be angry with you over that."

He moved to take her back into his arms. "Glad you see the big picture."

Kasey stepped back, eluding his movement. "But I can be angry that you went to see my grandmother and didn't tell me about it."

That caught him off guard. He glanced at Frank, who shook his head, denying any culpability for the leaked information.

"How did you…?"

Kasey pointed at the dead man. "He told me. He also said he had my grandmother's hospital room bugged and that he had some nurse on his payroll to keep tabs on my grandmother's visitors. I guess he expected me to show up." Kasey let out a shaky breath. "You should have told me, Zack. You should have told me you went to see her in the hospital."

"I made a judgment call. You had too much to deal with. I didn't want you to be overwhelmed."

She wanted to believe him. "So when were you going to tell me?"

"Soon." And then, because she was looking at him, waiting for him to follow that up with something more concrete, he added, "Probably when I tried to stop you from skipping town."

She didn't quite make the connection—other than the obvious one. "So you were planning on using that as a weapon?"

If she thought to embarrass him, she failed. "I was going to use anything I could to keep you from disappearing, yes."

"Why?" Why would he go out of his way like this? Why inconvenience himself as well as his brother? Yes, they'd slept together, but that wasn't enough to motivate a man to go out of his way like this.

"If you don't mind my butting in," Frank interjected, his manner clearly saying that he assumed he was being given a pass, "I think that's kind of obvious, don't you?" His words were clearly directed at Kasey, rather than the brother he was ignoring. The brother he was currently annoying.

"No," she replied.

"Butt out, Frank," Zack ordered sharply.

But it was too late for that. Frank continued as if Zack hadn't said anything.

"Well, it's obvious to the rest of us. The man is in love with you. I've never known him to give up his vacation time to sit in a parked car, voluntarily doing surveillance. Zack *hates* surveillance work."

"That's enough, Frank," Zack told him sharply.

It was Kasey's turn to be stunned. "Is it true? What Frank is saying, is it true?"

Zack shot Frank an annoyed look that told the younger man he'd deal with him later. "Well, I would have preferred that it had come out under more ideal circumstances, but—"

"Is it true?" she asked him again, this time more forcefully.

"Yes, it's true. I love you and I don't want to lose you." He looked over his shoulder at his brother, who was unabashedly watching and listening. "There, are you satisfied?"

Frank grinned. "In case this little detail escaped you, big brother, I'm not the one who has to be satisfied." He nodded toward Kasey. Just then, he cocked his head, listening. The faint bleating of sirens sounded in the distance. "Ready or not, here come the boys in blue," Frank announced. And then he became the professional again. "You can tell them you'll give your statement tomorrow if this is too much for you."

From the way he said it, Kasey gathered that he thought of her as fragile. Fragile wouldn't have seen her through her ordeal and fragile had no place in her life now.

She shook her head. "No, I'd rather get this over with tonight," she told him. "I want this all behind me as soon as possible."

"All?" Zack asked, wondering if she was about to sweep him out of her life after all.

A smile curved the corners of her mouth as she inclined her head.

"Most of it," she revised. "Most of it behind me." There was no way she was about to wish him out of her life—or do anything that would remove him, if she could help it.

"Better." Because he knew he had a limited amount of time before they were overrun by the police Zack made her a quick promise. "And from now on, there'll be no more secrets from each other. I promise," he added solemnly just in case she thought he was referring to the secrets she'd kept from him.

Guilt swept over her as Kasey thought of the life she was carrying. This was definitely not the most opportune moment to tell the man he was going to be a father, but then again, after he'd just said about no more secrets, she couldn't not tell him about this.

And if she didn't say anything and he should find out on his own, then he might never trust her again.

Opportune moment or not, he had to be told. She bit her lower lip. "Zack, I've got something to tell you."

Zack couldn't exactly say why, but he really didn't like the sound of that.

Chapter 15

But before Zack had a chance to step to the side with Kasey, several uniformed policemen came into the house, their weapons raised and ready.

"Easy, boys," Zack cautioned them in a low, soothing voice. He held up his badge, displaying it for all to see. "We're on the job. We're on the job," he repeated for good measure.

Slowly, the tension in the air abated. The patrolmen lowered their guns and holstered them.

The first one to enter, a redheaded six-foot-six rookie named Royce, looked as if he was about to ask Zack for instructions as to what he wanted done first when he stopped dead in his tracks. The rookie let out a long, low appreciative whistle. His eyes widened as he looked from the body on the floor to Zack. "Is that who I think it is?"

"All depends on who you think it is," Zack answered, doing his best to curb his impatience. He peered at the badge and added, "Officer Royce," to make the conversation seem more personal and hopefully bring it to a speedy end. Right now, he wanted to hear what Kasey had to tell him, not play twenty questions with a wet-behind-the-ears rookie.

"Carmine Pasquale." The large patrolman squatted down beside the body to get a closer look. "It is. It's the head guy himself." Rising again, he glanced at Zack, awe shining in his brown eyes. "You really bagged a big one, Detective. They said that this guy has—had—more lives than a cat."

"Looks like he finally ran out, doesn't it?" Frank commented from across the room.

More law enforcement officers arrived, cramming into the small house. Police personnel, people from the crime scene investigation unit as well as from the coroner's office all vied for space and elbow room. Two paramedics were the last on the scene.

"Sorry, boys," Zack said when he saw the two attendants making their way to the room, angling a gurney between them. "There's nothing left to resuscitate. All Pasquale needs now is a standard-issue body bag."

The lead paramedic stopped. "You're sure?"

"I'm sure," Zack responded.

The paramedic nodded, signaling for the attendant

behind him to go back and fetch the body bag. "Well, at least it saves on paperwork," he said philosophically.

Working his way around the gurney, Frank came to Zack, his hand extended toward the gun Zack still held. "I'm going to have to take your gun, Zack." He sounded apologetic. "Protocol."

Zack laughed shortly, surrendering the weapon. "Don't explain protocol to me, Francis. I'm the one who taught you, remember." Humor curved his mouth. "By the way, don't forget to hand over your own gun. There were two shots, remember? I only fired once."

"How do we work this?" Frank asked. "Do I give you mine?"

Zack laughed. "In this case, we hand them both over to the captain."

Kasey's eyes finally shifted from the figure on the floor. In death, Pasquale somehow looked even more menacing than he had in life. She shivered and ran her hands over her arms. If anything, the room was growing too warm from all the people in it. But inside, she was still shaking almost uncontrollably as if she'd never get warm again.

She tried to distract herself. "You have to surrender your guns?" she asked, puzzled.

Zack nodded. Police procedure wasn't exactly the topic he wanted to pursue with her. "IAB's way of keeping everyone honest and in-line. Every time we fire our guns, we have to account for the bullets."

Kasey shrugged, thinking he was describing unnecessary harassment. "That's easy enough," she interjected. "The bullets are in him."

"And then," he continued, hiding his amusement at her response, "if we shoot someone, it's up to IAB to determine whether or not it was 'a good shoot.'"

This was getting pretty involved and complicated, she thought. Unnecessarily so as far as she was concerned. Didn't the police department trust its own people? And then she thought of the detective who'd shot Jim. Maybe there were reasons to be suspicious.

"Meaning what?"

He slipped his arm around her shoulders. God, but it felt good just to hold her like this. He could have lost her tonight. If he hadn't looked up just then and seen Pasquale slipping in through the front door, she could be the one on the floor instead of the wise guy chieftain.

"That I didn't just shoot someone because I was having a bad day," he explained patiently, "or because I didn't like the way he parted his hair. There has to be the threat of imminent danger."

She took a breath, desperate to steady her nerves. They remained jangled. When was it going to stop? When was she finally going to feel calm? This couldn't be good for the baby. "Does keeping him from shooting me count as a good enough reason?"

A low, warm laugh rippled in his throat and he pressed a kiss to her forehead. "Most definitely." He wanted some time alone with her, if only a few minutes. He glanced over his shoulder at Frank. "Can you fill these guys in on everything?"

"No problem." Frank waved him on. "Get your girl out of here."

"Your girl?" Kasey echoed as Zack began to steer her past all the people who had come to fill her house. The paramedics were waiting to take the body, but the photographer from CSI hadn't finished digitally recording the scene yet. "Is that what I am?"

Reaching the front door, Zack opened it and took her outside. Privacy was at a premium out here, as well. Zack ushered her over to one side, out of the way of foot traffic.

Facing her, he told her, "I'm not sure how to answer that."

She'd come too far to back off. She needed to know. "Because you don't know how you feel about that?"

"No, because I don't know how you feel about the label. If someone called my sister Riley his girl, she would balk at that and say that it made her feel like property."

A small smile curved her lips. "So you're being sensitive to my feelings, is that it?"

He nodded. "Something like that. I don't want to risk upsetting you, especially after what you've just been through." Instead of responding, he saw Kasey pinch herself. "What are you doing?"

"Seeing what it takes to wake me up," she replied simply.

"Wake you up? Why? You're not asleep."

"Maybe not," she conceded, "but I am dreaming." And then her smile deepened. "Because you're too good to be true."

"That man almost killed you," he pointed out

sternly. "I think that alone would qualify this as a nightmare, not a dream."

"It's not a nightmare if someone rushes in to save me at the last minute," she corrected. She ran her palm along his cheek. Deep affection swelled in her chest. "Then it's a fantasy come true."

"Next time we'll play pirates," he deadpanned. "With rubber swords." He was relieved to hear her laugh, really laugh. Zack slipped his arm around her waist. "You were going to tell me something before the entire Aurora police department started pouring into your house."

She shook her head. Maybe now wasn't the right time. She had no idea how he was going to react to the news and for now she just wanted to savor being with him like this. "It can keep."

But he had seen the serious look on her face and had drawn his own conclusions. Conclusions that told him he wasn't going to like what he heard. Before she had turned his life completely upside down, he would have said fine and gone along with her decision to table whatever it was she'd been about to say. He would have had no desire to hear things better left unsaid. But that was the old Zack. The new Zack wanted to face life prepared. And if the news she was about to impart was bad, he wanted to know what it was so that he could find a way to turn it around.

He took his best guess about her unvoiced thoughts. "Now that you have your life back, you're going away, aren't you?"

Zack's question, completely off base, threw her. "What?"

"That's what you were going to tell me, wasn't it? Now that no one is out to kill you anymore, now that you're safe, you want to go back to pick up the threads of your life." And even as he said it, he knew that there was no way he was going to let her just walk away from him, not without putting up a damn good fight.

"Since you're so good at being a detective, you must know that all those 'threads' you have me going back to unraveled rather badly." There was nothing in Kensington for her any longer. Her life was here now—with a few minor changes. "Except for my grandmother, I have no reason to go back. And my grandmother could easily be persuaded to move to a city where the hospital care is superior to that of Mercy General. You've got some pretty first-rate facilities here."

The weight that had been pressing down on him vanished, just like that. "Then you're not going back to Kensington?"

"Is that disappointment I hear in your voice?" she asked, just barely able to keep a straight face.

"Are you crazy?" Overjoyed, Zack picked her up and enthusiastically spun her around.

"Hey, Zack, easy with our witness," Frank called out, seeing them through the window he'd just opened. "She's turning a little green on us."

Frank was right. The sudden motion had a very bad

effect on the perpetually unsettled pit of her stomach. Not to mention that her head was spinning, as well. She braced her hands on Zack's shoulders and urgently instructed, "Put me down."

The moment that he did, she made a mad dash back into the house, going straight to the bathroom.

Concerned, Zack quickly followed in her wake, only to have the bathroom door slammed shut in his face.

"Kasey, are you all right?" he demanded through the closed door. She didn't answer him immediately and he could have sworn he heard her retching, even if the sound was muffled by all the other noise that was abounding around him. "Kasey?" Worried now, he tried the door and discovered that she'd locked it. "Kasey, open the door. Open the door," he repeated. "Don't make me knock it down."

Finished with the coroner, Frank came over to his brother. "Hey, what the hell did you do to her?" he wanted to know.

"Nothing," Zack snapped. "She just—" He didn't get to finish. The door opened and Kasey stepped out. He'd never seen her face look so pale, not even when he'd rushed in earlier when Pasquale was after her. "My God, Kasey, you look whiter than snow." He took hold of her hand. "I'm taking you to the hospital to have you checked out."

She pulled her hand away. "There's no need to check me out," she retorted. She knew exactly what was wrong with her and it had nothing to do with having had her life in jeopardy.

Zack paid no attention to her protest. "This whole ordeal would have been a lot for anyone to handle. I can't even begin to imagine what you've been through. There's no shame in having your system suddenly rebel on you," he told her, believing that her pride made her stubbornly refuse hospital care. "They'll run a few tests, give you a once-over, see what's wrong. And I'll stay with you the entire time," he promised.

But Kasey shook her head. Again, she pulled her hand away from his. "There's no need for any of that. I know what's wrong with me."

"Look, just because you're a doctor doesn't mean you know everything."

"No argument," she granted. "But in this case, I do." It looked as if he was going to have to find out, even if this wasn't the proper place or time, she thought. Otherwise, he just might carry her off to the hospital, firefighter style. She turned toward his brother. At least she could try to secure a little privacy. "Frank, can you give us a minute?"

Frank instantly complied, backing away, his hands raised as if surrendering his right to any information. "I wasn't even here."

Taking Zack's hand, she drew him back outside, this time through the rear entrance. Where they had first encountered each other. Or, more accurately, where she had encountered him. As for his part, she doubted if Zack remembered anything about those first few minutes.

"Doesn't matter what you say," he addressed the

back of her head, "I'm still planning on taking you to the hospital."

Gathering her courage to her, she stopped walking and turned to face him. Her mouth instantly became horribly dry. She had to force the words out. Her voice sounded tinny to her ear.

"I'm pregnant."

Zack stared at her without saying a word. It looked, for a moment as if he'd lost the ability to process the English language or even understand it. Finally, his voice returned. "What did you say?"

"I'm pregnant," she repeated. "Don't worry, I'm not asking for anything. I don't expect you to—"

Zack suddenly snapped out of his trance as the import of what she'd just told him sank in. "Marry me."

She thought he was filling in the rest of her statement. "Right. I don't expect you to marry me or even to—"

"Marry me," Zack repeated as something akin to colored strobe lights began to flash and mingle inside of his head.

She was having a tough time ignoring his interruptions. Why was he doing this to her? Didn't he understand that she was trying her best to be fair to him and to the baby?

"—have any responsibility for the baby," she doggedly continued, "which I'm going to raise as—"

He grasped her by the shoulders in an effort to get her attention. She wasn't listening, he thought, frustrated and elated at the same time.

"Marry me," he said for the third time, more insistently this time.

Kasey stopped dead and looked into his eyes. "Are you asking me to—"

"Yes!" he almost shouted, desperate to get his proposal across to her. He was not prepared for her response.

"No."

He'd never asked anyone to marry him before. Never wanted to commit to anyone before. Now that he had, he'd assumed that the answer would be a positive one. He never thought he'd be turned down.

He felt numb. "What?"

Shrugging out of his grasp, Kasey squared her shoulders and repeated, "No."

Stunned, he could only stare at her. She loved him, he was certain of it. She'd even said so herself. Was it fear that kept her from saying yes? Or was it something else?

"Why?"

She could feel herself fidgeting inside. More than anything she wanted to say "yes." But she couldn't. He was asking her to marry him for all the wrong reasons. She refused to have someone marry her out of a sense of obligation. She couldn't live with that on her conscience. This wasn't the fifties or the sixties anymore. Plenty of single mothers out there. She'd just join their ranks.

"Because you don't have to."

"But I *want* to," he insisted. Didn't she know that? Couldn't she feel it?

"I don't want you to do this out of some kind of misbegotten sense of obligation," she told him, a surge of anger emerging out of nowhere.

"But it's not."

Did he think she was that stupid? With an angry huff, she drew him a diagram. "You didn't ask me before you knew about the baby."

But it had been on his mind, he admitted silently. It had been there for a while, taking shape, amid his thoughts. He probably should have said something, but he hadn't wanted to rush it. And he wanted to be sure. He was sure now.

Besides, there had been other things taking center stage up until now.

"You might have noticed I was a little busy trying to save your life." And then he looked down at her flat abdomen, a horrifying thought suddenly occurring to him. She'd been banged around a bit. "Pasquale didn't hurt the baby, did he?"

Despite her protests, his concern, his question, struck her as incredibly sweet.

"It's the size of an underdeveloped pine nut right now." She smiled. "Pasquale would have had to have gone in with a tiny nutcracker to do any damage."

That only put him slightly at ease. "You're still getting checked out," he insisted, then added, "After you say yes."

If he kept asking, she was going to break down and say yes—because she wanted to, more than anything.

But she still wasn't convinced that he wasn't doing it out of some old-fashioned notion of right and wrong. She'd already seen that he came from that kind of a family.

"Zack, really, you don't have to marry me," she insisted.

He put his arms around her and drew her closer. After a moment, she stopped resisting. "Yeah, I do."

"Why?" she asked again. As far as she was concerned, there was only one good reason to get married.

"Because I love you, that's why."

And that was it. Hearing him say it, really say it, left her stunned. "You love me?"

It amazed him that a woman as intuitive as Kasey was had missed this completely. "Of course I love you. Why do you think I've been sitting out there, watching your place every night when I hate surveillance? Having Frank tail you when I wasn't around?"

She pressed her lips together, feeling her will to resist ebbing swiftly away. "I don't know. Why?"

"Because I love you," he repeated, almost shouting the words.

The next moment, the back door opened and Frank stuck his head out. "We get it, Zack, you love her. Now move on and say something more romantic."

Zack frowned. Family or not, he didn't need these kinds of interruptions. "Shut the damn door, Frank."

Frank sighed, shaking his head. "Nope, that wasn't it."

"The door, Frank. Now!" Frank quickly withdrew,

complying. As the door closed again, Zack looked back at Kasey. He framed her face with his hands, as if he was trying to memorize all the contours of her face. "You saved my life, Kasey."

"I'm a doctor," she reminded him. "That means I'm supposed to—"

"I'm not talking about the bullet you removed. I'm talking about the heart you jump-started."

When he stopped, as if he was struggling with something, she said, "Go on."

He might as well tell her everything, he thought. He meant it when he'd said that there were to be no more secrets. "My father was an abusive man. He made my mother's life a living hell. I was afraid that I'd wind up being just like him no matter how much I tried not to be. But I never cared about anyone enough to test that theory. Never let myself care," he admitted. "And then you came along and I found myself caring a lot more than I thought was ever humanly possible." His mouth curved as he looked into her eyes. "Found myself loving a lot more than I thought I ever could—and not turning into my father. All I want to do is make you happy."

Her insides felt as if they were immersed in sunshine. "Well, you're certainly on the right road for that."

"Then you'll marry me?"

Her smile widened. "What do you think?"

"I think I'm still taking you to the hospital to check you out—later," he qualified as he lowered his mouth to hers. "A lot later."

"And can I call my grandmother on the way there?"

His lips all but brushed against hers as he said, "Absolutely."

And she was perfectly fine with that.

* * * * *

Don't miss Marie Ferrarella's next romance,
DIAMOND IN THE ROUGH,
available July 2008
from Silhouette Special Edition.

The editors at Harlequin Blaze have never been afraid to push the limits—tempting readers with the forbidden, whetting their appetites with a wide variety of story lines. But now we're breaking the final barrier—the time barrier.

In July, watch for BOUND TO PLEASE by fan favorite Hope Tarr, Harlequin Blaze's first ever historical romance—a story that's truly Blaze-worthy in every sense.

Here's a sneak peek…

BRIANNA STRETCHED out beside Ewan, languid as a cat, and promptly fell asleep. Midday sunshine streamed into the chamber, bathing her lovely, long-limbed body in golden light, the sea-scented breeze wafting inside to dry the damp red-gold tendrils curling about her flushed face. Propping himself up on one elbow, Ewan slid his gaze over her. She looked beautiful and whole, satisfied and sated, and altogether happier than he had so far seen her. A slight smile curved her beautiful lips as though she must be in the midst of a lovely dream. She'd molded her lush, lovely body to his and laid her head in the curve of his shoulder and settled in to sleep beside him. For the longest while he lay there turned toward her, content to watch her sleep, at near perfect peace.

Not wholly perfect, for she had yet to answer his marriage proposal. Still, she wanted to make a baby with him, and Ewan no longer viewed her plan as the travesty he once had. He wanted children—sons to carry on after him, though a bonny little daughter with flame-colored hair would be nice, too. But he also wanted more than to simply plant his seed and be on his way. He wanted to lie beside Brianna night upon night as she increased, rub soothing unguents into the swell of her belly, knead the ache from her back and make slow, gentle love to her. He wanted to hold his newly born child in his arms and look down into Brianna's tired but radiant face and blot the perspiration from her brow and be a husband to her in every way.

He gave her a gentle nudge. "Brie?"

"Hmm?"

She rolled onto her side and he captured her against his chest. One arm wrapped about her waist, he bent to her ear and asked, "Do you think we might have just made a baby?"

Her eyes remained closed, but he felt her tense against him. "I don't know. We'll have to wait and see."

He stroked his hand over the flat plane of her belly. "You're so small and tight it's hard to imagine you increasing."

"All women increase no matter how large or small they start out. I may not grow big as a croft, but I'll be big enough, though I have hopes I may not waddle like a duck, at least not too badly."

The reference to his fair-day teasing was not lost on

him. He grinned. "Brianna MacLeod grown so large she must sit still for once in her life. I'll need the proof of my own eyes to believe it."

Despite their banter, he felt his spirits dip. Assuming they were so blessed, he wouldn't have the chance to see her thus. By then he would be long gone, restored to his clan according to the sad bargain they'd struck. He opened his mouth to ask her to marry him again and then clamped it closed, not wanting to spoil the moment, but the unspoken words weighed like a millstone on his heart.

The damnable bargain they'd struck was proving to be a devil's pact indeed.

* * * * *

Will these two star-crossed lovers
find their sexily-ever-after?
Find out in BOUND TO PLEASE by Hope Tarr,
available in July
wherever Harlequin® Blaze™ books are sold.

Silhouette

SPECIAL EDITION™

NEW YORK TIMES BESTSELLING AUTHOR

DIANA PALMER

A brand-new Long, Tall Texans novel

HEART OF STONE

Feeling unwanted and unloved, Keely returns to Jacobsville and to Boone Sinclair, a rancher troubled by his own past. Boone has always seemed reserved, but now Keely discovers a sensuality with him that quickly turns to love. Can they each see past their own scars to let love in?

Available September 2008
wherever you buy books.

REQUEST YOUR FREE BOOKS!

2 FREE NOVELS PLUS 2 FREE GIFTS!

Silhouette® Romantic

SUSPENSE

Sparked by Danger, Fueled by Passion!

YES! Please send me 2 FREE Silhouette® Romantic Suspense novels and my 2 FREE gifts (gifts are worth about $10). After receiving them, if I don't wish to receive any more books, I can return the shipping statement marked "cancel." If I don't cancel, I will receive 4 brand-new novels every month and be billed just $4.24 per book in the U.S. or $4.99 per book in Canada, plus 25¢ shipping and handling per book plus applicable taxes, if any*. That's a savings of at least 15% off the cover price! I understand that accepting the 2 free books and gifts places me under no obligation to buy anything. I can always return a shipment and cancel at any time. Even if I never buy another book from Silhouette, the two free books and gifts are mine to keep forever.

240 SDN EEX6 340 SDN EEYJ

Name	(PLEASE PRINT)	
Address		Apt. #
City	State/Prov.	Zip/Postal Code

Signature (if under 18, a parent or guardian must sign)

Mail to the **Silhouette Reader Service:**
IN U.S.A.: P.O. Box 1867, Buffalo, NY 14240-1867
IN CANADA: P.O. Box 609, Fort Erie, Ontario L2A 5X3

Not valid to current subscribers of Silhouette Romantic Suspense books.

Want to try two free books from another line?
Call 1-800-873-8635 or visit www.morefreebooks.com.

* Terms and prices subject to change without notice. N.Y. residents add applicable sales tax. Canadian residents will be charged applicable provincial taxes and GST. Offer not valid in Quebec. This offer is limited to one order per household. All orders subject to approval. Credit or debit balances in a customer's account(s) may be offset by any other outstanding balance owed by or to the customer. Please allow 4 to 6 weeks for delivery. Offer available while quantities last.

Your Privacy: Silhouette is committed to protecting your privacy. Our Privacy Policy is available online at www.eHarlequin.com or upon request from the Reader Service. From time to time we make our lists of customers available to reputable third parties who may have a product or service of interest to you. If you would prefer we not share your name and address, please check here. ☐

SRS08R

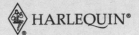

HARLEQUIN®

DOUBLE THE REASONS
TO PARTY!

**We are celebrating American Romance's
25th Anniversary just in time to make
your Fourth of July celebrations
sensational with Kraft!**

American Romance is presenting
four fabulous recipes from Kraft,
to make sure your Fourth of July
celebrations are a hit! Each
American Romance book in June contains a different
recipe—a salad, appetizer, main course or a dessert.
Collect all four in June wherever books are sold!

kraftfoods.com—
deliciously simple. everyday.

Or visit kraftcanada.com
for more delicious meal ideas.

www.eHarlequin.com

KRAFTBPA

Silhouette®
Romantic
SUSPENSE

COMING NEXT MONTH

#1519 A SOLDIER'S HOMECOMING—Rachel Lee
Conard County: The Next Generation
When he learns the truth about his father, military man Ethan Parish is determined to reunite with his long-lost family in Wyoming. On his way into town, he clashes with policewoman Connie Halloran, whose captivating beauty entices him. Together, they confront the dangers inherent in family secrets.

#1520 KILLER PASSION—Sheri WhiteFeather
Seduction Summer
Racked with guilt over his wife's murder, Agent Griffin Malone tries to get his life back on track. Enter Alicia Greco, an attractive and accomplished analyst for a travel company. The two meet and find passion, which is exactly what puts them into a serial killer's sights. Will they escape the island's curse on lovers?

#1521 SNOWBOUND WITH THE BODYGUARD—Carla Cassidy
Wild West Bodyguards
Single mom Janette Black needs to protect her baby from repeated threats by the girl's father. Fleeing for their lives, she knows bodyguard Dalton West is the only man who can help. After taking them in, they brave a snowstorm and discover a sense of home. This time, can Janette trust that she's found the perfect sanctuary...and lasting love?

#1522 DUTY TO PROTECT—Beth Cornelison
Crisis counselor Ginny West is trapped in an office fire when firefighter Riley Sinclair walks into her life. A bond forms between the two, especially when he keeps saving her from a menacing client. As danger still looms, one defining moment forces the pair to reassess their combustible relationship.

SRSCNM0608